VOLATILE VICE

BELLAMY BROTHERS FIVE

HELEN HARDT

HS
HARDT & SONS

This book is an original publication of Helen Hardt

This is a work of fiction. Names, characters, places, and incidents either are the product of the author's imagination or are used fictitiously, and any resemblance to actual persons, living or dead, business establishments, events, or locales is entirely coincidental. The publisher does not assume any responsibility for third-party websites or their content.

The author acknowledges the trademarked status and trademark owners of various products referenced in this work that have been used without permission. The publication/use of these trademarks is not authorized by, associated with, or sponsored by the trademark owners.

Cover Design: Shepard Originals
Edited by Eric J. McConnell

Print ISBN: 978-1-952841-36-1

VOLATILE VICE

BELLAMY BROTHERS FIVE

Helen Hardt

HELEN HARDT

WWW.HELENHARDT.COM

PRAISE FOR HELEN HARDT

"Literally perfection."

~**Read with Aimee** on *My Heart Still Beats*

"Helen Hardt is a master at making you fall for the bad boy."

~**Words We Love By** on *Savage Sin*

"Hardt spins erotic gold..."

~***Publishers Weekly*** on *Follow Me Darkly*

"22 Best Erotic Novels to Read"

~***Marie Claire*** **Magazine** on *Follow Me Darkly*

"Intensely erotic and wildly emotional..."

~***New York Times*** **bestselling author Lisa Renee Jones** on *Follow Me Darkly*

"Christian, Gideon, and now...Braden Black."

~**Books, Wine, and Besties** on *Follow Me Darkly*

"This red-hot tale will have readers fanning themselves."

~**Publishers Weekly** on *Blush*

"Scintillating..."

~**Publishers Weekly** on *Bloom*

"Helen's intelligent writing style and skills have made this story a must-read."

~**FireSerene Reads** on *Bloom*

"It's hot, it's intense, and the plot starts off thick and had me completely spellbound from page one."

~**The Sassy Nerd Blog** on *Rebel*

"This book was fantastic! It was steamy, funny, romantic, and just about any other emotion you can think of..."

~**Steamy Book Mama** on *Lily and the Duke*

"*Craving* is the jaw-dropping book you *need* to read!"

~***New York Times* bestselling author Lisa Renee Jones** on *Craving*

"Completely raw and addictive."

~**#1 *New York Times* bestselling author Meredith Wild** on *Craving*

"Talon has hit my top five list...up there next to Jamie Fraser and Gideon Cross."

~***USA Today* bestselling author Angel Payne** on *Craving*

"Talon and Jade's instant chemistry heats up the pages..."

~**RT Book Reviews** on *Craving*

"Sorry Christian and Gideon, there's a new heartthrob for you to contend with. Meet Talon. Talon Steel."

~**Booktopia** on *Craving*

"Such a beautiful torment..."

~**Bare Naked Words** on *Craving*

"Made my heart stop in my chest. Helen has given us such a heartbreakingly beautiful series."

~**Tina, Bookalicious Babes** on the Steel Brothers Saga

"A dark, intoxicating tale."

~**Library Journal** on *Unchained*

"Helen Hardt has some kind of skill I don't have the words to describe. Her writing is addictive. She sucked in my mind and I just don't want to read anything but her right now!"

~**OMGReads Blog**

"Helen Hardt...is a master story teller."

~**Small Town Book Nerd**

For Eric and Kaileigh

PROLOGUE

VINNIE

I wasn't completely honest with Savannah about why I went to the Buddhist temple.

It wasn't just to alleviate the guilt of leaving her and Mikey back in the States at the whim of the family. And it wasn't just to work through what my grandfather had done to me.

It was because I found myself involved in something far more sinister.

One fateful day, I ended up in a secluded alley in Prague, where a crooked wooden door creaked open to reveal an underground gambling den. There I met Misha—a man whose green eyes gleamed with dangerous amusement.

His real name was Mikhail, which threw me—the Slavic version of Michael. I thought of Mikey, who I'd left at home, and guilt overwhelmed me. When Misha offered me an opportunity to make a huge profit, part of me felt like I was talking to my brother, so I jumped in with both feet.

Misha was searching for a hidden treasure buried in the heart of Eastern Europe.

I was intrigued—and also desperate for some easy cash.

But it turned out not to be so easy. I dived into Misha's world, abandoning my odd jobs and my pursuit of quiet anonymity. He gave me a firearm but told me not to use it unless I had to defend myself.

A year passed. I lived in shadows and chased ghosts. Misha kept me busy while he sometimes disappeared for days at a time. His name notwithstanding, I didn't fully trust him, but I found myself enjoying the chase. Every time doubt crept in, Misha would return, always with a new clue, a new lead.

I got sucked in, and the whole thing became a game to me. Did I think we'd really find treasure? Maybe at the time I did. It gave me a creative outlet, something to do.

Until I realized it wasn't all that different from what I'd fled from at home.

I was becoming bound to a different kind of family. Not my mafia family, but an Eastern European underworld. Misha operated under different rules, but the principle was the same—secrets, power, betrayal.

I had to get out. But how?

One cold night in Bucharest, I got my chance, but it wasn't the way I imagined it.

Misha told me he'd uncovered the final piece of the puzzle, located within the grip of a rival gang. We'd need to be quick. We'd need to be strong.

"Are you afraid?" Misha asked me.

"No," I lied through gritted teeth.

"Good," he said. "Fear will only lead to your demise."

The gang had set up their base in an old chateau. The

stone structure was imposing as hell and full of foreboding darkness.

As we moved through the corridors, our footsteps muffled by the worn-out rugs, my heart pounded. The echoes of raucous laughter and clinking glasses reached us, growing louder with each step we took. Misha led the way. He was in his element. Danger was his drug.

Until he turned on me.

To this day I don't know why. Maybe because I presented a challenge to him. Maybe he decided he wanted all the loot for himself. Or maybe he was just batshit crazy.

But that night, I had to do something I swore I'd never do.

I took a life.

It was self-defense, but I still had to move quickly and quietly to avoid being caught.

I learned to travel during the night. Change my appearance when necessary.

And I was done with crime.

Done.

Until now, of course.

If everything went according to my plan, Puzo should be dead.

He was a piece of shit, and the world won't mourn him.

But doing my grandfather's bidding doesn't give me the revenge I crave.

The vengeful vice I've been carrying around with me since that fateful day in his office, where he violated me in the worst way while I refused to scream out in pain.

Because fuck him.

Fuck him and fuck the world that allowed him to exist. I left that life behind, buried it deep under layers of pseudonyms, fake passports, and never-ending roads. But the ghosts were always there, whispering in my ear, reminding me of all that had been taken from me.

I existed in the shadows, a phantom flitting through Europe. I eked out a living doing odd jobs, never staying in one place for too long. As long as I remained a ghost, I was safe.

But I'm back now.

And I'll have my revenge.

I regard Raven. She's sleeping soundly.

It kills me to leave her, but she has no place in the world I have to inhabit.

I can't shake the anger coursing through my veins. Every time I close my eyes, I see Misha's face, smirking, laughing as he turned on me.

He's not laughing now.

Grandfather thinks I'm weak. Too weak to take Puzo out with a gun he provided.

That doesn't make me weak. It makes me smart.

Grandfather doesn't know who he's dealing with. But he will soon enough.

Vengeance isn't just a fleeting thought for me. It's my driving force, my vice. It consumes me, and I welcome it.

Every step I take is fueled by the need to make Grandfather pay. I've lost so much because of him, and now it's my turn to take something. It won't bring back what I've lost, but it will satisfy this burning need inside me. He thinks he's untouchable, but his arrogance will be his downfall.

I'm a storm ready to unleash hell. He won't see it coming until it's too late. I'll be his reckoning. I'll be his nightmare. And when it's done, maybe then I'll find some peace.

Or maybe this vengeful vice will have consumed me completely, and there will be nothing left but the ashes of my own destruction.

But until then I will be relentless. Nothing will stand in my way. They will regret the day they crossed me. This isn't just a promise. It's my reality, my unyielding obsession.

I didn't mean to fall in love.

I didn't mean to drag an innocent woman into my underworld.

I press my lips to Raven's soft cheek.

Then I rise from the bed, dress quietly, and leave.

Never to see her again.

1

RAVEN

The sun cascades through my window as I wake up. I rise, throw my legs over to the side of the bed, stretching my arms over my head.

Vinnie and I had sex last night.

Correction. We made *love.*

He said he loves me. And I told him I love him.

God, I don't know if I've ever been happier.

I look around. He's not here. Odd. I throw on a robe. Maybe he's an early riser, got up to make a pot of coffee.

I saunter into the kitchen, yawning. "Vinnie?"

But he's not here.

Maybe he had an early meeting with that grandfather of his. Certainly he'd have left me a note, though, right?

I'll check my phone. Maybe he left me a text.

I turn on the screen. No texts at all since last night.

Including from Brick. I check to make sure the text I sent him canceling our date went through. It did.

He was probably pissed at me for flaking at the last

minute. I can't blame him. I sigh. I guess I'll have to find another lawyer to help me out with the nonprofit.

But Vinnie didn't text me, which is weird.

I put the phone down. I'm about to start a pot of coffee when it rings.

It's my mom. Damn it. I didn't text her last night to let her know I'd be spending the night at my place. She'll be beside herself with worry.

"Hello?"

"Oh Raven, thank God."

Mom's voice is high-pitched and energetic. I can hear a lot of hustle and bustle in the background. The house seems very active for early in the morning.

"Yeah, I'm sorry I forgot to call you last night."

"Are you at your place?"

"I am."

"Thank God." Mom's voice is still pretty frantic.

My heart begins to race, but I'm not sure why. All I know is something isn't right here.

"Is anything the matter?" I gasp. "Is something wrong with Dad?"

"No, sweetheart. Your father and I are fine. But we..." She lets out a hysteric sob.

"Mom, what's wrong?"

But she can't seem to get herself together. Something is very wrong here.

"Can you put Dad on?"

Mom blubbers out some words I can't make out, but then I hear my dad's voice on the receiver. "Raven. Didn't you have a date with that lawyer last night?"

"I did." The guilt hits me again. "But I... I wasn't feeling too great, so I canceled it."

Dad's tone is artificially even. "Did you cancel it at the very last minute?"

"I did."

"I see." Dad pauses. "Your mother and I went to a movie last night. We got back late and went straight to bed. This morning, she got up to check on you, and..."

"What, Dad? I wasn't there? I'm sorry, I should have called to—"

"No, it's not that." Dad clears his throat. "She found... someone else in your bed."

My blood runs cold. "*What?*"

"Yes." Dad pauses. "It was...a body."

My heart is pounding out of my chest. "A body? Like...a *dead* body?"

"Yes." Dad's voice is shaking through the phone. "The lawyer. Mr. Latham. His throat slit wide open."

Oh my God, oh my *God...*

"There was a note on your nightstand next to him. Handwriting I don't recognize."

A note? Oh God, did he kill himself? He seemed pretty level-headed. Surely a broken date wouldn't be something that would drive him to...

There's no way.

I draw in a shaky breath. "What did it say?" I whisper.

I can hear Dad shudder from the other end of the line before he finally speaks again.

"*Your move, Cobra.*"

Cobra? Fear surges through me. What does that mean? How did—

"How... The house... How..."

"Somehow the security system was disarmed," Dad says, his low voice a monotone. "It's state of the art. I don't know how it happened."

My father's voice sounds...unsure. Unsure and frightened. And my father never sounds unsure and frightened. Even when I was sick, he kept his strength. He never let me see his fear for me. He knew I needed him to be strong.

And now...

Everything comes back to me in a swarm of memories.

The Uber driver. The phone call to Vinnie. The burner phone with instructions—the phone I still have. Telling Vinnie about everything in my backyard. The dark drone flying above us. And then him leaving.

Fear envelops me. When Vinnie was here, I wasn't feeling fear. I was feeling comfort, safety.

Love.

But now that he's gone...

I'm ready to be back on my own. But not before I have a professional come to my house and make sure there's absolutely no surveillance equipment here.

I have a state-of-the-art alarm system, too. If someone got through my father's system, they could surely get through mine. I was right to ask Vinnie if we could speak freely. If someone *is* watching me—so they can be watching Vinnie—they're the kind of people who can easily get around any alarm system.

I want to go home now.

I want to get out of this house until I know it's safe.

But Mom and Dad's house isn't any safer. It's less safe. Brick was killed there. Had his throat slit there. I shiver, trying to ease the chills by rubbing my arms.

Doesn't work.

"All right," I say, willing my voice not to shake. "I'm coming home, Dad. I'm coming home."

"I don't want you driving alone. I'm coming to get you."

I swallow. "No, it's okay. I'm okay."

"You stay put. I'll be there in ten. Do not move, Raven. Do. Not. Move." The line clicks off.

I crawl back on my bed, clutching my knees to my chest.

Poor Brick... If only he'd gotten my text in time.

If I'd remembered to text him earlier, he wouldn't have shown up at my house at all.

But as horrible as I feel about Brick, I'm equally ecstatic that Mom and Dad were out for the evening. What if my father was the true target? What if...

And why did Vinnie leave in the middle of the night without waking me?

I grab my phone again and dial Vinnie.

Only to get his voicemail.

I open my mouth to say something, but no words emerge.

I can't bring myself to tell him that Brick is dead in my bed.

I can't...

No.

Not until I see it.

I have to see it.

My mom and dad wouldn't lie to me, but still...I have to see it.

Why didn't Vinnie answer?

I clutch my knees again, shaking.

And feeling completely and utterly alone.

2

VINNIE

Several hours earlier...

I don't drive home to my mother's home. Or my grandfather's.

Instead, I changed into the clothes I left in my rental car —dark denim jeans and a black hoodie. A black baseball cap on my head, thin cotton gloves that I'll put on later. In the middle of the night, I drive to Houston—to the hotel where Giacomo Puzo should now be dead in his room.

The Carlton Deluxe Downtown is the most expensive hotel in Houston.

Nothing but the best for Puzo and his Colombian deals.

I walk in, my heels clicking on the marble tiles of the lobby. To the right, a grand chandelier casts a golden glow over an elegant seating area adorned with plush velvet sofas and intricately carved wooden tables. A sweeping staircase with a gilded railing spirals up to the mezzanine level. In the center of the lobby stands a magnificent floral arrangement bursting with exotic blooms and rich greenery.

The reception desk is manned only by one impeccably

dressed staff member at this late hour, but he smiles as I enter and walk toward him.

I've never met the man, but I know him.

He matches the description of the person I've paid off.

I clear my throat. "Raul, I presume?"

"Yes." He keeps his face noncommittal. "You're Mr. Brown?"

I nod. He knows very well that my name isn't Mr. Brown. Who I am doesn't matter. What I'm about to do does.

He slides a key card to me. "Here you go. Room 1027, tenth floor."

"Much obliged." I pull out my wallet, slide the key card in, take out two crisp hundred-dollar bills, and slide them to Raul.

He nods back.

Then I walk through the ornate lobby to the elevators, slide the gloves on, and press the button.

The doors open for me right away. It's the middle of the night, and very few people are using the elevators.

I walk inside, making sure to keep my face away from the surveillance equipment.

This isn't my first rodeo.

I slide the key card over the reader and hit the button for the tenth floor.

In a flash, the elevator doors open, and I walk out, following the signs to room 1027.

I hover my card over the reader, and when I hear the click, I open the door.

This is Puzo's room. He should be lying dead somewhere, and I'm here to make sure everything went off without a hitch.

I have no personal beef with the man, but he has to die. He has to die so I can regain my grandfather's trust. Without that trust, I won't be able to bring him down.

Once the door is securely closed behind me, I blink a few times, letting my eyes adjust to the darkness. "Puzo?" I say softly.

Once I can see, I realize I'm in a suite. This is the living area. Probably where he ate his meal—the meal that was supposed to be laced with peanut butter. The allergy that will kill him. His EpiPen should've been taken from him by another one of my operatives.

This is the second time I've killed. The first was with my own hand—Misha overseas.

This one? I kept my own damned hands clean.

But I don't kid myself. I'm responsible for this man's death. My only consolation is that he seems to be a real dirtbag.

I walk through the living room of the suite. The remains of Puzo's meal sit on the dining table. A dark rectangular takeout container. Completely empty, with a fork on the table beside it. Next to it a paper bag with the words *Mister Noi's Thai* written on it.

I'm not sure which part of it was laced with peanut butter, but it doesn't really matter. It appears he ate it all. I bring the takeout container to my nose and sniff it. It's mostly the smell of curry, but there's a slight tinge of peanut butter.

Good. This hotel doesn't let food couriers go up to the levels beyond the lobby to make deliveries. They have to leave it at the front desk and a bellhop brings it up to the guest's room. The bellhop was then instructed to take the bag discreetly aside and then mix in a few tablespoons of peanut butter—the smooth kind, of course.

One of the odd jobs I performed when I was hiding from my grandfather in Europe was food delivery. It always struck me how insanely trustworthy you have to believe your delivery drivers are. Usually they have total access to your food before you receive it.

Finding no sign of him, I walk through the doorway into the bedroom. Two queen beds—and neither has been slept in.

Where the hell is he, then?

God, I hope he didn't stumble out of the room and flag someone down for help. That would ruin this whole thing, and I'm already on thin ice with my grandfather as it is.

"Vincent," he'll say. "You should have taken matters into your own hands. The way I told you to."

Shit. I really don't want to have to deal with that.

But then my eyes fall on the one room I haven't seen yet. The bathroom.

I slowly slink toward the closed door. Puzo could very well still be alive. Or in anaphylactic shock. I might have to snag one of the pillows off the bed and finish him off the old-fashioned way.

Grandfather would like that.

I knock on the door. "Sir? I'm from housekeeping. The front desk sent me up to do a wellness check."

No answer.

I slowly open the door. It's not locked, thank God.

But it's dark. I hit the flashlight on my phone.

Damn, this is a nice bathroom. I guessed Puzo likes to shit in style.

Liked to shit in style, hopefully.

The light bounces off of richly veined marble walls and gilded mirrors outlined with crystal sconces.

Fuck. No one's in here.

I shine my light around. There's a clawfoot tub fashioned from gleaming copper and polished porcelain standing majestically in the center, accompanied by a rain shower enclosed in frosted glass. I look inside the shower, and it's empty. Nothing here is amiss, except...

A pile of silver-capped toiletries—luxury-brand shampoo, conditioner, lotion, and shower gel—litter the floor in front of the marble countertop of the grand vanity. These would normally be stacked neatly by the housekeeping staff, but it looks like someone rushed by them quickly and let them fall to the floor.

And then I see a carved wooden screen, which must conceal the toilet.

I slowly inch toward it, and a foul smell emanates from the area. I peak around the privacy screen.

I know what to expect, but my breath still catches when I see a body hunched over the porcelain toilet. The bowl is filled with vomit, and even in the darkness, I can see the gray pallor of Puzo's face and hands.

I take a good look at his eyes. Shine my flashlight into them.

There's no sign of life.

I grab his wrist, feel for a pulse. Nothing there, either.

Yes. It's Puzo.

And he's dead as a fucking doornail.

The plan worked, and he's gone.

Next time I won't have to identify the body myself.

I may not have shot him in cold blood like my grandfather wished, but I took care of the situation. Other than Raul, I paid off the bellhop who delivered his food and one of the maids to secure his EpiPen.

All trustworthy people—if willingness to help kill a man for money counts as trustworthy—according to my resources.

Still...something pricks at the back of my neck.

If I'd simply shot him like my grandfather asked, I wouldn't have had to involve others. I wouldn't have to depend on their discretion.

But doing it this way? Yeah, there are a few potential loose ends, but I was far away from this venue when it happened.

My hands are clean. My alibi is secure.

And I'll make sure that the three people who helped me continue to be handsomely rewarded.

I move to leave when I remember.

The pinky ring.

The gawdy thing my grandfather hates. I hate to admit it, but he's right. It's a thick gold band textured like gold nuggets with a huge star sapphire in its center.

He wants Puzo's pinky, but no way in hell am I sawing off his finger. I grab the ring and shove it in my pocket. I exit the bathroom and head back into the living area of the suite.

Then I leave the room, walk calmly to the elevator, again making sure to keep my face down as I saunter through the hollow hallway and get into the elevator.

Once I'm back on the first floor, I leave—this time through the back door.

Only then, once I'm in my rental car, do I allow myself to ponder the magnitude of what I've put into motion.

Nausea overwhelms me.

Because this isn't who I am. No matter what I did overseas—no matter what I did this evening—this is *not* me.

I need to remember that.

Because things are about to get volatile.

And that's the only way I'll be able to do what needs to be done.

I'll walk the path of darkness. Dip a toe into the shadowy realm dominated by men like my grandfather.

But I can't allow myself to completely fall down the rabbit hole.

Because if I do?

I'll never be able to escape.

3

RAVEN

It's Hawk—not my father—who picks me up at my house.

"Ray?" His voice echoes through to my room.

"In the bedroom."

I'm still clutching my knees.

He peeks inside and widens his eyes when he sees me. "You okay?"

I close my eyes. "How'd you get in?"

"The system wasn't armed." He crosses the room and sits on the edge of my bed.

I slap my palm to my forehead. "How could I be so dumb?"

After everything I've been through, I forgot to turn on my security system. Vinnie wouldn't have been able to leave in the middle of the night if I had. What was I thinking? What was *he* thinking?

I suppose we both had a lot on our minds. Not that I'm going to clue my younger brother in to that facet of my personal life.

But one thing is for sure. I'm having this place checked out right away.

Hawk leans down and brushes my upper arm. "It's all going to be okay, Ray."

Okay. This is the exact opposite of *okay*. And I don't see any way of making what happened to Brick in my bed—the bed I slept in through the bulk of my childhood—okay.

I burst into tears, throwing my arms around Hawk's broad shoulders. "Oh, Hawk, I don't know what to do!"

"Easy." He rubs my back. "Everything's going to be okay, Ray."

"How can you say that?" I wipe my eyes. "Mom says Brick Latham is dead. In my bed!"

"I know." He squeezes my shoulders. "But you're *here*. You weren't there. You had nothing to do with it."

I pull back. "Of course I had nothing to do with it. You didn't think—"

He shakes his head quickly. "Of course not. No one does."

"Mom and Dad..."

"They're okay. They got home last night and didn't even notice until this morning."

I grab a tissue from my nightstand and blow my nose. "We should have a dog."

"What?"

"A dog. Sam was a great guard dog. When I got sick and Mom and Dad had to take care of him during my hospital stays—"

"Raven, please. Be glad they *don't* have a dog right now. Whoever did this would have just killed it."

"Oh, God." I fall back into Hawk's arms. Then I pull back again. "Do you think this has anything to do with Diego—"

He holds his fingers to my lips. "Shh." He looks around my bedroom. "I don't know, Ray. I just don't know. Come on. Let's go."

~

I ARRIVE to the police at our home, my own bedroom full of people.

And on the bed?

A zipped-up black vinyl body bag.

I gulp.

At least I don't have to look at the body of Brick Latham—that nice man who was helping me with my nonprofit foundation. Who only wanted to take me on a date last night.

Why would anyone harm Brick?

My heart sinks into the pit of my stomach like a heavy stone dropping into the icy depths of an unending ocean. I stumble, nearly falling as the officers turn to look at me. My mother is there, her face bleached to a sickly white and her eyes rimmed with red.

"Mom?" I ask, my voice barely a whisper. "Where's Dad?"

"He's out back talking to our attorneys on the phone." She points a shaky finger out the door. "Hawk went out there."

"Is Dad talking to one of the attorneys from Brick's—Mr. Latham's—firm?"

She shakes her head. "I don't know, Raven. I just don't know."

I need to call Vinnie.

He'll know what to do.

Won't he?

He didn't answer when I tried before. Maybe he was in a

meeting or something, and I didn't leave a voicemail. I didn't —couldn't—say any of this out loud.

I fumble for my phone, my hands shaking. I press Vinnie's name and hold the phone up to my ear, my heartbeat thumping a wild manic beat. The ring echoes in my head.

I look around at the police officers whispering among themselves and at my mother who is now huddled in a corner talking in hushed tones with a tall man in an expensive-looking suit. The body bag on the bed seems out of place in my room. My favorite band posters still hang on the wall and a few books are scattered about. There are stuffed animals on a shelf next to my bed, and boxes full of DVDs of old comfort-food movies that I used to escape my illness.

The body bag has poisoned everything in my room.

I can never sleep here again.

I walk into the hallway, keeping the phone pressed to my ear.

But Vinnie still doesn't answer.

Again, I hear his away message. And again, I can't bring myself to leave a voicemail.

The man talking to my mother walks toward me. "Raven Bellamy?"

"Yes?"

"This is your bedroom?"

"Yeah." I swallow. "I'm staying here. Sort of. I was at my own place last night. But I'm recovering from leukemia, and I..." The words just stop, caught in my throat.

"Yes, your mother told us." He pulls out a pad of paper. "We need to ask you a few questions."

I simply nod.

"In the living room, maybe?" the man says.

"Sure." I swallow.

"I'm Detective Harris," he says. "Jeremy Harris."

"Raven Bellamy." But he already knows that. What's wrong with me?

What's *not* wrong with me would be a better question.

We head into the living room. He gestures me to have a seat. Mom sits next to me.

I sit on the edge of the couch, gripping the cushion beneath me as if it could anchor me to some semblance of reality. The room feels too bright, the morning sun streaming through the windows stark and unforgiving. Detective Harris stands in front of me, his notepad open. Another officer, Joel Martinez, stands by the door.

"Ms. Bellamy, can you walk me through your evening?" Detective Harris asks, his voice calm but with an undercurrent of suspicion.

I swallow hard, trying to steady my racing thoughts. "I was at my house last night," I begin, my voice trembling slightly. "It's on the ranch property, about ten miles from here."

"Were you alone?"

My lips tremble. Do I tell them I was with Vinnie? That we saw a drone flying above us in my backyard? Is it all related somehow?

I suppose it's best to tell the truth.

Vinnie would tell me to tell the truth.

Wouldn't he?

"I spent the evening with a friend."

"And this friend can verify you were with her?"

I blink. "Him. I was with him. And yes, he can."

"His name, please?"

"Vincent Gallo, Jr."

Mom goes rigid next to me. I'm not sure how much they know about Vinnie's family. Do they even know Falcon was beaten within an inch of his life and almost killed by Miles McAllister? Has Hawk told them? Falcon and Savannah aren't here. Do they even know what's going on yet?

Harris takes notes. "Okay. I'll need his contact information."

I grab my phone because I haven't memorized his number. I rattle it off. "He left in the middle of the night, though, and I haven't been able to get hold of him since then."

Harris lifts an eyebrow but continues taking notes. "All right. Do you know what time he left?"

"Honestly, no. I wasn't looking at the time. I mean, I was asleep at that point. We..."

How much detail does he want? What happened between Vinnie and me was personal, and I don't want to talk about it to strangers. And certainly not with my mother sitting right here.

"Take us to this morning, then."

I nod. "I received a call from my mom this morning, around seven. I had just woken up—that's when I realized Vinnie had left—and I was making coffee when my phone rang. Mom said she found a body in my bed here." I glance toward the hallway leading to my bedroom, the image of the scene my mom described flashing in my mind. I'm again grateful that I didn't have to see Brick's body with his throat slit. Seeing his blood all over my bed was bad enough.

"Did you know the deceased?" Harris asks, his pen poised over the notepad.

I gulp. "Yes, his name is Brick Latham. He's a lawyer. We had a date last night, but I canceled at the last minute. Maybe he didn't get my text in time." I hold up my phone. "You can see the text here. Anyway, he was helping me with some legal paperwork for a charitable foundation I want to create."

Harris narrows his eyes. "Did you invite him here last night?"

"Yes." I frown. "Except no. I broke the date. But even if he didn't get my message in time, he wouldn't have been able to get in the house. My mom and dad were out." I turn to Mom. "Where was—"

"I already told the detective that all the staff had last night off," Mom finishes for me. "They usually get Friday nights off anyway, and we didn't think it necessary for them to stay if we were going to be out late."

"Can anyone confirm that you were at your house all night?" Harris presses, his tone making it clear he's not convinced.

I begin to feel defensive, but I hold myself in check. This isn't the time.

"Vinnie can, at least until he left. I was at my house the entire night. I didn't come back here until my mom called me this morning."

Detective Harris nods, jotting down notes. "When was the last time you saw Brick Latham?"

"A few days ago, here at my parents' house. We met to discuss the charity paperwork. That was the last time."

"Did he mention anything unusual? Was he acting strange or did he seem worried about anything?"

I close my eyes, trying to recall our conversation. "No, he seemed fine. We talked about the charity, his work, just normal things. He didn't mention anything that seemed out of the ordinary."

"Did you notice anyone watching you or following you recently?" Harris asks, his gaze unwavering.

Do I dare mention the Uber experience?

On a whim, I shake my head. "No, not that I can remember."

Harris exchanges a glance with Officer Martinez before turning back to me. "Ms. Bellamy, do you have any idea who might want to harm Mr. Latham?"

The question sends a chill down my spine. I think of Vinnie, of the dangerous world he's part of and the threats that seem to shadow us. But I can't bring that into this. It has nothing to do with Brick, anyway.

"No," I whisper, my voice barely audible. "I don't know who would want to do this. I don't know why anyone would do such a terrible thing."

"All right." Harris says, closing his notepad. "We may need to take your statement formally down at the station. For now, if you remember anything, no matter how small it might seem, please let us know."

I nod, feeling numb. "I will."

Detective Harris turns to my mother and then to my father, who's now standing in the entry to the living room. His lips are pursed.

"Mr. and Mrs. Bellamy, can you explain again where you were last night?" Harris asks, his tone measured but firm.

Dad clears his throat, glancing at my mom before speaking. "We were out for dinner and a movie. We got home late, probably around midnight. We didn't check Raven's room because we assumed she was already in bed."

"And you didn't notice anything unusual when you got home?"

"No," Mom says, her voice shaky. "We went straight to bed. This morning, I went to check on Ray, and that's when I..." She chokes back a sob.

"Why didn't you hear anything during the night?" Martinez asks, narrowing his eyes.

"Our bedroom is on the other side of the house," Dad explains. "We didn't hear anything unusual."

Harris and Martinez exchange a glance, and then Harris turns back to me. "Ms. Bellamy, we'll be in touch. And remember, if you think of anything else, please contact us immediately."

"Jeremy," Dad says, "your father and I have known each other for years. Talk to him. He'll tell you we had nothing to do with any of this."

"I'm well aware of your standing in this community, Mr. Bellamy," Harris says. "I'm just doing my job."

As they leave, a hand touches my shoulder. I turn to see my mom, her face etched with worry and fear.

"We'll get through this," she says softly. "We'll find out who did this."

I lean into her, drawing strength from her presence. "I hope so, Mom. I really hope so."

Because frankly? I'm scared out of my wits. I still don't know where Vinnie is or why he left. And I'm not even sure I'm safe in my own home.

My father no doubt knows experts in the security field. I could probably get someone out to look at it today. But no way am I going to ask my father. Not after what he and Mom have been through. I'll call Falcon. His friend Leif Ramsey knows security better than anyone.

"I talked to Steve Palmer," Dad says. "He says to cooperate with the investigation. He didn't seem too worried."

Mom rises. "I think we could all use some coffee. And breakfast."

God. The thought of food... But Mom is right. I have to force something down. I didn't even look in my kitchen when I left this morning. The spaghetti marinara I made for Vinnie last night is probably congealed and disgusting by now. We didn't eat it. We went straight to bed after the drone incident.

My God, what is happening in my life?

I haven't eaten since the sandwich I had at noon yesterday at my house.

I stand. "Sure, that would be great. Two scrambled eggs and—"

"Toast," she says. "You've got it, Raven. And I want you to drink a big glass of orange juice for me, okay? You need your vitamins."

I nod, even though I hate the stuff. "Of course, Mom." I follow her into the kitchen.

I get what she's doing. She's committing to her routine. Trying to stay with familiar things to get her mind off the horror. Who can blame her?

She pulls a pitcher of OJ out of the refrigerator, pours a large glass, and sets it on the table. "Sit," she says.

I obey her, but my body does not want to sit. My nerves are having a field day under my skin. I feel like I need to keep moving. Except that I don't want to keep moving. I want to crawl up on my bed inside a blanket and forget everything.

But I won't succumb to that.

I spent enough time curled up on my bed worrying about my life ending while I was sick.

I need to embrace my life. And that means embracing these fears. Getting through them. As soon as I'm done with breakfast, I'll call Falcon. I'll have him and his friend Leif meet me at my house. They'll make sure my place is safe. And I'll have them make sure this place—my parents' house—is also safe.

I down the orange juice, knowing I will be in heartburn city in a moment. But it makes my mother happy.

What I really want is a can of Orange Crush. I'm an adult. I should be able to have what I want. But right now I don't want my mother to be more upset than she already is. I didn't mean for any of this to happen. It was always my intention to come home. And if I had, I'd have found...

God...

But at least that would have been better. We'd all have alibis.

If only Vinnie hadn't left in the middle of the night. Then I'd have an ironclad alibi as well.

I scroll absently through my phone, looking for some message from him. No texts, no missed calls. He's not on social media.

I have no idea whether he's dead or alive. And with Brick dead? Anything could have happened to Vinnie.

Your move, Cobra.

What the hell does that even mean?

I try to swallow the lump in my throat, but to no avail.

My mother brings my breakfast over to me with a forced smile. "Here you go. Just how you like them."

I force a smile back at her. "Thanks, Mom." The eggs are poached instead of scrambled. Poached eggs are gooey, and Mom knows I hate them. She'd never make them for me if she was herself.

I can't bring myself to draw attention to her mistake. Instead, I push my fork into one of the poached eggs, swirl it into the yolk, and dip a toast point in the yellow liquid. I bring it to my mouth, but the smell...

Normally I love eggs. Especially the fresh eggs we have here on the ranch.

But the smell of it. The taste of it—

I gulp, trying to dislodge the lump in my throat, and I take a bite, chew, force it down.

The second bite is easier. The third bite is about the same. Mom will worry if I don't eat, and I do need sustenance to keep my strength and aid in my recovery.

I'm not going to add to the turmoil of this morning.

So I eat all of it. All of the breakfast.

Now what?

Mom is standing over me like a shadow.

"How are things going at your house?" she asks. "Are you getting it livable again?"

Classic Mom again. Trying to ease the tension with conversation. "Yeah. I've missed it."

"I know you have, honey. It won't be long before you're back there full-time."

Right. Not until I have a security system that's worth a damn. And not until there's one installed here as well.

I rise. "Thanks for breakfast. I have some work to do. You know, with the foundation I'm putting together and all."

"Oh, yes. How's that going?"

Well, I no longer have a lawyer, but...

"So far so good. I don't have anything to report yet. I need to start working on fundraising."

She gives me a half-hug around my waist. "You know your father and I will do everything we can to help. Including financially."

"I know that, but I don't think you have to. I'm using some of my own money, and Robbie is investing as well."

"I'm glad to hear that." She sighs. "I wish we saw more of Robin. For someone who works right here on the ranch tending to our animals, she doesn't come around a lot."

"That's just Robbie," I say.

And I'm thankful she's not here for this.

"Yes, she never was the homebody that you are."

I force another smile and then leave the kitchen.

I can't go to my bedroom. It's a fucking crime scene.

So I go outside on the deck and call my brother.

"Raven?" he says into the phone.

"Hey, Fal."

"Oh my God, what's the matter? You don't sound good."

"A little freaked out, to be honest."

"Why?"

My heart skips a beat. "No one told you what happened?"

A pause. "Ray, what's going on?"

I take a deep breath in. I haven't actually verbalized what happened to Brick to anyone. I tried to leave a voicemail for Vinnie twice, but I couldn't get the words out. And I spoke as little as I could when the detective was interviewing me.

"You know that lawyer I told you about? The one who's helping me with the nonprofit?"

"The one you had a date with?" His voice suddenly

adopts an edge. "Did he do something to you? Did he hurt you?"

"No, no. It's nothing like that. I actually canceled the date. I...wasn't feeling well."

"What happened, Ray?"

"He..." I choke on the words. I swallow and force them out. "He's dead, Fal. Someone killed him. And they left the body in my bed."

No response.

"Fal? You there?"

"Is this some kind of joke?"

"I swear it isn't. On Mom and Dad's life. It's awful. They have no idea what happened." The emotions spring back out of my throat, and tears start falling down my cheeks again.

"Hey, hey." His voice evens out. "What matters is that *you're* okay, Ray. Mom and Dad are okay."

I wipe my eyes. "I suppose."

"I can't believe something like this would happen at their house, though. Why didn't anyone call me?"

"Mom and Dad called Hawk to pick me up at my place this morning. I guess they didn't want to bother you. I mean, you've been through so much and all."

"Fuck..."

"But you're right. I'm okay. Mom and Dad are okay." My stomach twists into a sailor's knot. "I can't say the same for Brick Latham."

"I'm on my way."

"No," I say. "Please. You and Savannah need to—"

"Damn it, Ray, I'm still a member of this family. I'm coming over."

"Fine. Come over. In fact, call Leif. I need a favor."

"What for?"

"I've been back at my house the last couple of days. Trying to get ready to move back in."

"Already?"

"Yeah. I need to get back on my feet. But the issue is..."

God, how do I even say this?

"Yeah?"

"I need Leif to come take a look. Do a sweep. Make sure no one has been... I don't know..."

"Raven, do you think someone's watching you?"

"Maybe. Someone killed Brick, and Brick was coming to see me. And last night I had a feeling... You know that feeling you get when you feel like you're not alone?"

"Yeah, I know it all too well. You learn how to be hyper-aware when you're in the slammer. Believe me."

"God, Falcon... This is why no one wanted to call you. You've been through enough."

"Hey, it's over. And thanks to Vinnie, we have time to deal with everything else so that I don't go back."

Goosebumps erupt on my body. "Should we even be talking like this? On this line?"

"Probably not. Tell you what. I'll get Leif, and we'll meet you at your place. About an hour. Will that work?"

My mother will no doubt question me about where I'm going, but I want this done as soon as possible. "Yeah, that will work fine. See you then."

4

VINNIE

"It's done," I say to my grandfather as soon as I sit down in the chair facing his desk in the morning.

"Yes, I got word."

I keep my eyebrows fixed, resisting the urge to let them fly off my forehead.

Don't show surprise.

Never show surprise to my grandfather. Of course he was watching me. I'd be a fool to think otherwise. That drone last night at Raven's place? That was all him. When I texted him to call it off, it went away.

I toss the pinky ring on his desk. "Here's your prize."

He takes the ring, examines it. "What about the rest?"

I shake my head. "I'm not mutilating a dead body. I got the ring. Take your token. That's it. I got it done, and I did it my way."

He fiddles with the ring, a glint of something—oh God, I think it's pride—in his eyes. "I have to hand it to you, Vincent. It was a good idea. You did your research, and you figured it out." He puts the ring down and stares into my eyes.

"But not everyone I assign to you is going to have a peanut allergy."

"I'll find another way."

"You will also find," he says, completely ignoring my comment, "that when you take care of it yourself, with no witnesses, you keep yourself much safer."

"You've had plenty of witnesses over the years."

He cocks his head. "And how would you know that? You haven't been here."

"My father's an excellent resource," I say. "He's told me what I need to know."

"Your father's a fucking jailbird, Vinnie. A murderer."

I can't help it then. I let out a laughing scoff. "You know as well as I do that you've killed way more people than my father ever has. You also know that you could get him sprung in the next two minutes if you wanted to."

He presses his lips together. "You think I have that kind of power?"

"I *know* you do." I get to my feet. "You've told me yourself. The only reason my father's rotting in a prison cell is because you've got some deal going with the McAllisters. Declan McAllister won't give you peace unless my father's rotting behind bars for killing his son. But how many people has *he* murdered? How many people did Miles McAllister murder before he was killed? It's so fucking ironic."

Grandfather frowns. "The thing about irony, Vincent, is that it often strikes when you least expect it, especially when you think you've gotten away with something. Just when you've been lulled into a false sense of security, the universe will crash down to remind you in the most surprising way that it never forgets."

I'm quiet for a moment as I let my grandfather's words sink in.

For a moment I'm not sure they even came out of his mouth.

"And has the universe forgotten everything *you've* done, Grandfather?" I ask.

Silence as I wait for him to respond.

Just when I think he's going to completely ignore my question—

"I don't concern myself with the universe."

"Then why did you make the comment?"

"Because"—he clears his throat—"you need to be ready for whatever happens. Because you need to have a plan for every contingency, just in case the universe decides to bite you in the ass. The more people you involve in your mission, the better chance that something will go awry."

"So when you say you don't concern yourself with the universe, you're saying that never happens to you?"

He leers over the desk at me. "I'm saying, Vincent, that when it *does* happen to me, I take care of it. I have a plan in place for every eventuality."

I sit back down and think for a moment. What could go wrong? The clerk at the hotel. The maid. Perhaps a camera caught me checking things out early this morning.

That's unlikely, as I kept my face shielded at all times from any surveillance.

The same clerk I paid to give me the room key was also instructed to erase any surveillance tape.

Those are my only loose ends, and I've paid handsomely to tie them up neatly.

"Everything's been taken care of," I say, my tone sounding more confident than I actually feel.

"For your sake," he says, "I hope it is. Because if it's not?" He shakes his head. "This is all on you, Vincent. You'll need to take care of anything if the universe decides to come calling."

I regard my grandfather. For a man in his eighth decade, he's in excellent shape. But his eyes betray him. Not just the wrinkles around them but their color. Once nearly black, they're now faded like old leather. They hold a depth of stories, secrets carried through the years. In them, I see the weight of wisdom and a trace of sadness, witness to all he has seen and perhaps lost. Yet they remain windows to a soul that refuses to bow to the years. He has an act put on. The tough Mafia leader.

But he's getting old, and he and I both know it. His men know it.

"You can trust me. You can trust me to get things done my own way."

"Only time will tell on that, Vincent." He looks down for a moment before meeting my gaze again. "Don't think for one second that I will ever forget your betrayal. That I'll ever forget that you walked away from this family. That I'll ever forget—"

I stand. "And don't think for one moment, Grandfather, that I will ever forget what *you* did to me. What you did to Michael. What you wanted to do to Falcon Bellamy. And that you're allowing my father to rot in prison when you could get him sprung tomorrow. Don't think for a moment that I'll forget that you sold your own daughter into marriage."

He scoffs. "I sold her to your father. He turned out to be a big disappointment."

His response rings odd to me. I expected him to state the obvious—that if he hadn't sold my mother off to my father, I wouldn't exist. Neither would Savannah.

"Because he killed Miles McAllister?" I say. "Because he tried to save Savannah from the same fate as your own daughter?"

"Because he's weak," Grandfather says. "My only consolation is that my blood—" He closes his mouth abruptly.

"That your blood what?"

"My blood flows through *your* veins, Vincent. Don't ever forget that."

How I wish I could.

I rise, placing both of my hands on his desk. "How many other men and women have you violated, Grandfather? I can't imagine you were faithful to my grandmother all those years."

He says nothing.

Which tells me everything I need to know.

I regard him again. It's eerie how much I resemble him. How I favor him and my mother, while Mikey and Savannah favor our father.

Genes are funny things.

I clear my throat. "You need to stop having me followed."

"I'll stop having you followed when I'm good and ready." He scowls. "Did you really think some cheap rental car and cash would keep you undercover? Did you really think I wouldn't know that you were with Raven Bellamy last night?"

"My personal life is none of your business."

"It is when it interferes with *my* business. What if I had insisted that she be your target? What if I hadn't reneged?"

"Then I would've left this family again." I sink slowly into my chair. "I will not murder an innocent young woman. A woman who's already been through hell and has never done anything to hurt this family."

He smiles then—and in that moment, I can almost see scales forming on his skin. His tongue slithering out at me like a snake.

Maybe I'm the cobra, but he's the King Cobra.

If he ever finds out how much I care for Raven...

Would he take her just to punish me?

Yes. He would do it without hesitation, which is why I left her last night. And why I can't see her again.

She'll haunt me until the day I die, but until I can get my grandfather out of the picture, we cannot be together.

"I will do my duty," I tell him. "I'll do the duty that Mikey couldn't. I'll do the duty in payment for Savannah's freedom. For my mother. But I will *only* do it if you can guarantee Raven Bellamy's safety."

He scowls. "I don't make guarantees, Vincent. A man in my position doesn't have to."

"Then I'll get twenty-four-seven security on her."

He laughs at that one. And it's a serpentine laugh, as if it's coming from the throat of a rattler. "You think there's anyone you can get who I can't pay off?"

I draw a breath and let it out slowly, forcing the anger curling at the back of my neck to dissipate to the point where I can at least speak calmly.

"She's been through hell. She wants to start a nonprofit

foundation for blood cancer research. Let her have that. Let her have her life."

A small grin cracks across his face. "That, dear grandson," he says, "depends on you."

5

RAVEN

I still haven't heard from Vinnie.

I brush my upper arms against the chill as Falcon and Leif scrutinize every part of my home.

I don't have a phone line. Leif starts with the obvious spots, sweeping a device over the bookshelves and behind picture frames. The device emits a soft beep, and Leif pauses, removing a framed photograph to reveal a small, inconspicuous camera nestled behind it. He deftly disables it, nodding to Falcon.

Falcon moves to the kitchen, carefully inspecting the ceiling light fixtures and appliances. He finds a tiny microphone hidden inside a wall clock and signals Leif. Together, they disable it and continue their search.

In the bedrooms, they lift mattresses, check inside air vents, and even dismantle lamps to ensure no device goes undetected. I heave a sigh of relief when they leave my bedroom, finding nothing.

The thought of them having video footage of...

I can't go there.

Falcon finds another camera in the hallway cleverly disguised as a smoke detector, and Leif deactivates it.

Their search extends to the bathrooms, where they inspect behind mirrors and inside exhaust fans. Nothing there either, thank God. In the study, Leif examines the computer for any tampering, while Falcon checks behind the curtains and inside a decorative vase.

I follow them through my home, feeling more violated with each device they uncover.

Finally, they move to the outdoor areas, inspecting the porch lights and garden ornaments. They discover a hidden camera inside a garden gnome, which Falcon promptly destroys.

Nothing in the pool house, and nothing in the little alcove where the gazebo is. I guess Vinnie and I could've stayed there last night.

Nothing also around the fire pit, nor around the furniture where we ended up sitting.

I swallow hard. "I can't thank you enough," I say to Leif.

"You know I would do anything for your family," he says. "I will tell you that this is not hard-core monitoring."

"When did it happen? How could they get in here without anyone's knowledge?"

"These kind of guys are known for their discretion. They could have come in while you were sleeping and gotten these in place. But my best guess is that they set this up while you were still in the hospital," Leif says.

"But I had my security system armed."

Leif frowns sympathetically. "Unfortunately, your basic security system is nothing to experts. I'll get you set up with something better."

"Right away," Falcon says.

Leif nods. "We're going to need to check out your parents' place too." He turns to Falcon. "Your place is clean for now."

Falcon crosses his arms. "Can you guarantee it stays that way?"

"We'll set you up with the best system. Same as I'm going to do here for Raven. We'd best do it for Hawk and Eagle too, based on...you know."

"You can speak freely," Falcon says. "Raven knows everything."

I swallow again. "I don't want any of my family in danger."

"There's no reason you'll be in danger," Falcon says. "You had nothing to do with what happened eight years ago. This thing with Latham can't be related."

I bite my lower lip, looking to the ground.

"Ray..." Falcon begins.

I look up and meet his gaze. "There's something you should probably know."

"Fuck," he says. "What is it?"

Mom already knows because she was there during the questioning. She's probably told Dad by now. I can only imagine how he feels about it. "I've been..." I run my hand over my peach fuzz, letting it skim over my fingertips.

As much as I hate my lack of hair, it's actually a nice feeling. Kind of soothing.

"Raven," Leif says, "you're going to need to be honest with us if we're going to make sure you're protected."

I sigh. "I've become...involved with Savannah's brother."

"Vinnie?" Falcon shakes his head. "For Christ's sake, Ray. I like the guy, but he's a freaking mobster."

I shake my head. "He's a *fake* mobster. He's trying to take his family down. You know that as well as I do."

"I know, but being anywhere near him puts you in danger. I can't have that. Not after we almost lost you." He runs his hand through his hair. "And now that lawyer turns up dead. In your bed, Ray. This must have something to do with Vinnie."

Leif sighs. "I've got to agree with your brother. You're better off staying far away from Vinnie Gallo. But on the other hand..."

"What?" Falcon says.

"You say she knows everything, Fal?"

"She does. She heard the guys and me talking."

Leif shakes his head. "She may be in danger anyway, then."

"No," I say. "Vinnie took care of it. My father's guys can't dig there. The EPA is making them jump through a bunch of hoops."

"But don't you see?" Leif says. "That's the problem. The EPA is now involved. But not just the EPA. Bad guys in the EPA." He shakes his head again.

Chills course through me.

"I..."

"What is it, Raven?" Falcon demands. "You know I love you, sis, and I'm so glad you're still here with us, but you have to be honest with us."

"He left me," I say succinctly. "It's embarrassing, but he left me last night. We fell asleep, or at least *I* did, and when I woke up in the middle of the night, he was gone."

"He just fucking left you?" Falcon's hands curl into fists.

"Ease up," Leif says. "My guess is he's trying to protect her as well."

Falcon unclenches his fists, but I can see he's still rigid.

"I swear to God, Raven," he grits out. "I will die before I let anything happen to you."

I shake my head. "That's not what I want. You've been through enough, Falcon. You went to prison to protect our youngest brother. You've done your time. You and Savannah deserve happiness. Not to be pulled back into this."

"I love Savannah," he says. "And with Savannah comes her family. I knew what I was getting into with her. But you... You don't need this, Ray."

But I love him...

The words don't make it out of my mouth. Besides... Though he claimed to love me as well, he left without so much as a kiss goodbye. I haven't heard from him at all today despite calling him twice.

"I think it's probably a moot point," I finally say. "I guess he got what he wanted from me and took off."

There go Falcon's fists again, and this time Leif joins him.

"I don't mean that the way it sounds. I... I took from him as well."

Falcon begins to open his mouth, but I hold up a hand to stop him.

"Let me have my say, Falcon."

He sighs and nods.

"The thing is, during the last couple years I never thought anything like that would happen for me again." A surge of emotion runs up my throat. I swallow it back. "But Vinnie... He showed me that I'm still beautiful, even without hair—"

"Of course you are," Leif snaps. "You and Robin are gorgeous, no matter what."

I resist rolling my eyes at his mention of Robin. Leif and Robin were an item back in high school, and I don't know exactly how it ended because Robin doesn't talk about it. Leif is now happily married to a woman named Kelly.

"For Christ's sake, Leif, let me have my say too."

He nods.

"He gave me something I didn't even know I needed," I say. "I know you don't like hearing that about your sister, Fal, but I don't regret what happened between Vinnie and me. Not for an instant. And if he's gone on his way now, I won't try to stop him."

"Good," Falcon says. "I want you safe, Ray. And that means staying far away from Vinnie Gallo."

I look at my feet. "It's pretty clear he made that decision for me."

"What if he didn't?" Falcon asks. "What if something came up and he had to leave, and he just didn't want to bother you? What then?"

I don't want to lie to my brother. Because the fact of the matter is that I'll go back to Vinnie in an instant. I'm in love with him. And yeah, he lives in a dangerous world, but the idea of going through the rest of my life without that same feeling that he gave me...

So I lie. I look my brother in his dark eyes and I lie.

"Then I'll tell him to get lost," I say. "I'll tell him I don't want him, and I never will."

6

VINNIE

"How the hell does it depend on me?" I demand, still standing over my grandfather.

"Maybe I need to tell you a little story," he says.

"Please spare me."

"Sit down, Vincent. And hear me out."

I suck in a deep breath, counting to ten. Then I take my seat again, opposite my grandfather.

"Once upon a time—"

"Oh, for the love of God..."

"Shut up, Vincent. You're younger than I am, stronger than I am, maybe even smarter than I am. But I've got something you don't have." He narrows his cold, dark eyes. "The wisdom of a lifetime lived. I'm about to share some of that wisdom with you."

"Fine," I huff, resisting an eye roll.

"I was young once. Younger than you. There was a time, believe it or not, when I wanted to leave the family."

I open my mouth to speak but he holds up a hand.

"Please. Let me finish."

I widen my eyes. Did my grandfather just say please?

"So," he continues, "I decided I might be the one to leave. That I might be the one to break away. And you want to know why?"

"Not particularly."

"Jesus Christ, Vincent. Believe it or not, I'm trying to help you here."

"Fine. Go on. I won't interrupt you again."

"Damn right you won't." He closes his eyes and takes a deep breath before continuing. "I was promised in marriage to a woman much younger than me. Your grandmother. I was in a situation much like you find yourself in now, although I was younger than you are. I was twenty-five years old, and my betrothed was fifteen. We were to marry when she turned eighteen. But during those years, I was young. Young and full of life and—to put it crudely—horny as hell."

Oh God. Do I really have to hear about my grandfather's sex life?

"I met a young woman. Her name was Serena Deville. She was twenty-two years old, had just finished college, and had a vision. She wanted to change the world."

Change the world? Who the fuck *doesn't* want to change this world? But I stay silent.

"She was so vibrant and full of life. Beautiful too, with the palest blond hair and the brightest blue eyes I'd ever seen."

Grandfather closes his eyes then, and a look of—is it serenity?—crosses his face. I can't imagine my grandfather ever being serene. But something softens his face.

"Our meeting was anything but romantic. She was walking down the street, not looking where she was going with her nose in a book, and she ran into me. Her book fell to the ground. I reached down, picked it up, and handed it to her."

"Is this a real story or a scene out of a romantic comedy?"

He ignores me.

"When I looked into her eyes... I just knew." His eyes soften in a way I've never seen them before. "She was someone I needed in my life. Then she smiled at me, thanked me for picking up her book, and apologized for running into me. I knew I shouldn't, but I had to see her again. So I asked if she'd like to get a cup of coffee." He pauses.

Just when I'm about to say something he starts talking again.

"My father found out we were seeing each other. He told me to let her go. I told him it was just sex. I was using her. After all, I couldn't touch my intended until she turned eighteen. It was not as if I was expected to remain chaste until our wedding. But your grandfather—"

"You're my grandfather."

He clears his throat. "Your *great*-grandfather knew. He knew it was something more. He knew I had developed feelings for Serena. Feelings that got in the way of the business we did. Feelings that threatened my place in the organization."

He stops again.

Already I know what's coming.

"I refused." His entire body deflates slightly. "And I suppose you can guess what happened next."

"She was taken care of?"

"Worse, Vinnie. Much worse."

I wait, expecting him to go into detail.

But he doesn't.

Instead— "She was my Achilles' heel, Vincent. She weakened me. How I wish I could say she was only taken care of. But no, my father saw that she suffered. Made sure that I knew every little detail. And I learned that the only way to survive in this family was to harden myself. Build a wall around my heart. Do what was expected of me and do it well. Marry your grandmother and become the leader of this organization I was born to be." Then he scoffs. "Of course your grandmother was a huge disappointment to me."

"Because she only gave you one child?"

He frowns. "Only one, and a daughter at that. I hated her. Not just because she couldn't bear me sons, but because she wasn't Serena. I lost the love of my life, Vincent. But I should never have had that love in the first place. That was my mistake." He looks me straight in the eye. "Don't make it yours."

"We're two different people, Grandfather."

He holds up a finger. "All people are different, Vincent. But know this. If Raven Bellamy—or any woman other than your intended—is keeping you from doing your best for this family, trust me that I *will* have her taken care of. And be glad that I have more of a heart than my own father did. Death will be a mercy to her."

I say nothing.

Does he expect me to feel sorry for him? After all the grief he's caused? All the havoc he's wreaked? What he did to me? To Mikey? To my grandmother? To countless others?

So he had a great love. So what?

He could've fought for her. He could've left the country like I did. Hell, I'd still be there if not for Savannah. I came back for her. Of course in retrospect, I wish I'd come back for Mikey too.

"So you're telling me that you were actually capable of emotion at one point in your life?" I say.

He crosses his arms. "You think so little of me, Vincent."

I roll my eyes. "You're right about that."

"I'm not asking for your pity or your sympathy."

"That's good, because it won't be coming anytime soon."

"The point of the story is—"

I rise again. "I'm not an idiot, Grandfather. I know the point of the story. Stay in line, or you'll kill Raven. That's the point. And I'm supposed to be grateful to you that you'll just kill her instead of putting her through whatever torture they did to your *great love*, Serena." I stare him down. "Well, I've got news for you. I'm sure Serena was an innocent in all of this. I'm sorry she had to go through whatever hell your father put her through. But don't tell me you haven't done the same to others or worse. Because it will be a lie, and we both know it."

With that, I turn to leave the office.

"Vincent?"

I look over my shoulder. "What the fuck is it now?"

"Do not defy me. You may have won this first battle. But you have yet to gain my trust."

I turn around then, walk to the other side of his desk, and pull him out of his chair. "You listen to me, old man. You want me to run this family? Then you have no choice but to trust me. I will *not* keep jumping through hoops. You told me to take care of Giacomo Puzo, and I took care of him."

"You did so indirectly, and in doing so involved several other people."

"You're right. I didn't put a bullet between his eyes as you would've had me do. But I took care of the problem in much the same way that I'm sure you've taken care of problems over the years. You don't want me heading the family? I'll leave the country tomorrow. Then who do you have?" I tighten my hold around the scruff of his shirt. "I came back. I came back so Savannah could have a life. I came back to take my place. But you, Grandfather, have to *let* me take my place. You won't live forever. At some point you have to trust me."

"Let go of me, Vincent."

I keep hold of his collar.

He chuckles. "Do you think this makes you big and strong? Using your obvious physical power over an elderly man?"

I let go of his collar and push him back into his chair. "I don't think of you as elderly, Grandfather. And be honest with me. You don't think of yourself that way either."

Grandfather adjusts his tie. "I'd like you to join me for lunch today."

"What? We're just done with this conversation now?"

"I have a meeting." He looks at his watch. "And then I want you to join me for lunch."

I sigh. "Fine. Where and when?"

"At the McAllister house. We will be joined by a special guest."

"Fine. Who?"

He smirks. "Your intended. Declan's daughter, Belinda."

7

RAVEN

By lunchtime, Leif and Falcon have a security team at my house. It will take them the rest of the day to install the top-notch security system. I fix us a lunch of turkey and avocado sandwiches. At first I thought I'd heat up the leftovers from my date with Vinnie last night, but the marinara from last night is ruined.

"I want you to have someone here living with you," Falcon says.

"You mean like a live-in maid?"

He shakes his head. "I mean like a live-in bodyguard."

I open my mouth to protest, but then I think about it. It's probably not a bad idea.

"You have someone in mind?" I ask.

"I can get you a guy," Leif says. "I've got contacts. Plus I've done work as a bodyguard myself."

"I'd feel a lot more comfortable with you, Leif," I say.

"I think we'd all feel more comfortable," Falcon says, "but Leif's a newlywed. I don't think Kelly would relish him moonlighting as your bodyguard."

"No, I guarantee you she wouldn't." Leif nods. "Don't you worry, Raven. I'll find you someone just as good—or better—than I am."

I sigh. "When are you going to do Mom and Dad's house?"

"Probably tomorrow," Falcon says. "And I don't want Mom around for it. It'll just freak her out. I want you to get rid of her for the day."

"How am I supposed to do that?"

"I don't know. Ask her to take you into Austin for shopping. Or if you don't want to go that far, say San Antonio. You're not supposed to drive longer than twenty minutes, right?"

"Shopping? I don't need anything."

Leif laughs. "Since when does a woman need anything to go shopping?"

I dart him a glare. Robin may have been the tomboy when we were growing up, but she's the shopper now. I hate shopping. I hate going out in public looking the way I do.

But whatever. I'll do what I need to do.

"Fine," I relent. "I'll ask Mom to take me shopping tomorrow." I scratch the side of my head. "What should I say we're looking for? Buying clothes would be stupid when I'm finally putting back some of my weight."

"Nix the shopping then," Falcon says. "Tell her you want to spend some time with her. Go into San Antonio for lunch. Maybe see a movie."

I think for a moment. "There is that new Matt Damon movie I've been wanting to see. We could catch a matinee."

"There you go," Leif says. "Perfect."

"How long do you need?" I ask.

"At least four hours," Leif says. "Your parents' place is bigger than this place, so it's going to take a little longer. My guys are excellent, as you can see."

"All right. Lunch in San Antonio and then a movie. I think I can get Mom on board. Right now she's going to do anything to keep me happy and secure and safe."

"Right," Falcon says, "and she won't want you driving to San Antonio by yourself."

"Yeah. That's probably how I'll have to put it. I'm planning to go into San Antonio for lunch. And to see a movie, and she won't want me alone." I let out a short laugh. "Her helicopter parenting has now been put to good use."

"She's only worried about you, Raven."

"She didn't helicopter *you* while you were in prison."

"My life wasn't in danger in prison." Falcon's gaze darkens. "I made sure of that. And it's not like she had a choice. They don't just let your mommy come to jail with you."

I can't help another laugh. For having been through so much, Falcon has kept his sense of humor like a pro.

"Why don't you go ahead back to Mom and Dad's, Ray," he says. "You can start working on Mom about tomorrow. I've got this covered for you."

"Don't you have to get home to Savannah?"

"Savannah's good. She's busy checking out law schools online."

"That's great! She can finally fulfill her dream."

Falcon smiles. "I hope she can figure out a way to do it. It would probably require driving to Austin every day or if not, doing everything online."

"That's the way of the world these days," I tell him. "I bet there's a way she could drive in a couple days a week and then take the rest of her classes online. Maybe I'll go back to school myself."

Falcon raises his eyebrows. "I thought you were set on your nonprofit?"

Nausea crawls up my throat. "After Brick..."

"That's not your fault, Raven."

I close my eyes and swallow. "He was coming to see *me*. How do I know that I wasn't the target? And that he was just killed as a message?"

"I don't know," Falcon says. "We're going to make sure everyone's taken care of."

"I don't want to live my life like that, Falcon." I run my fingers over my fuzzy head. "I... I'm finally free of my disease. And who knows if it might recur? I want to live every day to its fullest, and that does not mean imprisoning myself inside a house."

Falcon stares at me.

"Oh, God... I shouldn't have used that word. Imprison."

Falcon frowns. "You don't have to walk on eggshells around me, Ray. I spent eight years in the joint. Everyone knows it. God knows I'll never forget it. But I'm out now, and I get what you mean exactly. Every day is a gift. I don't want to be locked up any more than you do."

I sigh. "I just can't allow these people to scare me. If I stay away from Vinnie, maybe they'll let me go."

"Do you *want* to stay away from Vinnie?"

Leif is talking to one of the security technicians. Only my brother will hear my answer if I care to give him the truth.

I bite my lip. "I'll be honest with you, Falcon. No, I don't want to stay away from Vinnie."

Falcon rubs at his forehead. "Do you want to stay alive?

Because you almost lost your life once, Raven, and none of us are prepared for that to happen again."

It's an interesting question. One that is killing me slowly. Vinnie Gallo may indeed be the love of my life. I've certainly felt things with him that I've never felt before. I'm nearly thirty years old. I'm not a little girl. I've been around the block several times, and I've never felt what I'm feeling with Vinnie.

On the other hand, I just got my life back. I spent the last few years wondering if I would live to see another day, and now that I know that I will, I don't want to give that up either.

What would it do to my family? Mom and Dad? To my brothers? To Robin?

And to Vinnie?

I swallow. "I want to stay alive, Falcon. I didn't fight this hard to die a young woman."

"That's exactly how I feel, Raven." A small smile creeps across his lips. "You and I have something in common."

"Yeah, our bone marrow." I let out a nervous chuckle.

He laughs. "Yes, that. But also, we had part of our lives stolen. Now we've got them back, and it's time to live. And not just for today either. Live for the next fifty years, Raven, because that's how long we both have."

8

VINNIE

I've created a new definition of nauseating awkwardness.

It's sitting next to your grandfather in a huge-ass living room, across from the eleven-year-old girl you're supposed to take as your wife seven years down the pike.

Declan McAllister sits next to his daughter, Belinda.

Belinda looks every bit the eleven-year-old girl. No signs of puberty yet. Just a little girl dressed in what can only be described as a pink party dress complete with ruffles and lace, white bobby socks, and black patent-leather Mary Janes.

All I can see is Savannah.

Savannah, who was ten years old when I left the country. She looked a lot like this little girl. No body shape yet, nothing to indicate she would one day be a woman.

Belinda sits with her hands in her lap, not looking at any of us, including her own father.

Grandfather and I are each nursing a bourbon. Declan drinks Irish whiskey. And Belinda?

A Shirley Temple.

Jesus Christ.

A Shirley fucking Temple.

Grandfather and Declan are discussing business. Nothing super detailed, of course. There's a child present. Just a few odds and ends. I listen intently, acting as if I care.

I nod, give a grunt of approval every now and then.

When they're finally finished, McAllister clears his throat. "We have a special treat for you, gentlemen. Belinda has just perfected the Chopin waltz in C-sharp minor. She would be honored to play for you."

"Of course," Grandfather says. "And we will be honored to hear it, won't we Vincent?"

I force a smile. "Absolutely."

Belinda rises from the loveseat where she sits next to her father and walks over to the black lacquer Steinway. She sits down on the bench daintily, and she closes her eyes for a moment. When she opens them, she places her fingers on the keys and begins to play.

I don't know anything about music, but her playing is excellent, to my ear at least. She's playing from memory, as no music is sitting in front of her.

I've heard this piece before. I'm not sure where, maybe from a commercial. It's in a minor key, so it has a certain somberness to it. But it still has the lilting three-quarter time of a waltz. Belinda's fingers, perfectly curled, fly over the keys as she plays a series of runs up and down the scale. Then the music shifts to a more hopeful major key for an all-too-brief moment, before another series of runs brings us back to the dark theme where we started.

Just like this damned business I've gotten myself into. No matter how good things can get—and with Raven, things got pretty freaking good—I always end up in the dark tonality of my grandfather's shadow. Never escaping. It's like Chopin wrote my fucking life story.

When she's finally finished, she closes her eyes for a moment and then lifts her fingers from the keys.

McAllister begins to clap, and Grandfather and I follow suit.

Belinda rises, walks toward us, gives a short curtsy.

Grandfather nudges me. This means I'm supposed to say something to my future bride. This little girl before me.

Again I force a smile, although I'm not sure why I bother. She hasn't looked at me once, and I can't blame her.

"That was lovely, Belinda," I say. "How long have you been playing the piano?"

"Since I was five," she says.

I nod. "It's pretty amazing. I don't know much about music. But it sounds like you're playing at a virtuoso level."

"Oh, she is," McAllister says. "Belinda is quite the prodigy. We don't have any musical talent in our family either, so we were really surprised when her kindergarten tutor brought her talent to our attention."

"Oh?" I say. "How did that happen, Belinda?"

Still standing in front of me but not looking at me, she says, "There's a piano in all the classrooms at my private school. Or there used to be." She looks at her feet. "I don't go there anymore. One day, I just sat down at it and started to play something."

"What did you play?"

"Just a tune I had heard on TV."

"And you figured out which notes were the right ones? Without any training?"

She nods slowly. "It was like sounding out a word you don't know."

"That's fascinating."

"Indeed it is," McAllister agrees. "We found out she has perfect pitch, and that she can play by ear. Simply hear something and then sit down and play it."

"But how did you know which keys to use?" I ask her.

She shrugs. "I figured it out."

Damn. This little girl has a talent. She's a prodigy. And her father's hope is for her to marry a man over twenty years her senior and be an obedient little Mafia wife.

So many things wrong with this picture.

"Mr. McAllister." The housekeeper enters, interrupting us.

"Yes, Dena?"

"Lunch is served.

"Thank you." McAllister rises and holds out his hand to Belinda, who curls her little fingers into it. "Come. Dena has prepared one of Belinda's favorites. Shepherd's pie."

Shepherd's pie? A hot meal during summer in Texas? Well, at least this house has perfect air-conditioning.

We follow McAllister and Belinda into the large dining room.

Four places are set. One at the head of the table, where I assume McAllister will sit. Then two on his left and one on his right.

Belinda scrambles into the seat next to her father on the right.

"Vinnie," McAllister says. "You sit next to Belinda, and Mario, you're here next to me."

Awkward just got a million times worse.

But I keep my forced smile on my face. Am I supposed to hold up the chair for her?

Thank God McAllister does it.

It's okay for a father to hold out a chair for his daughter.

For a thirty-four-year-old man who's supposed to marry her once she's legal?

Not so much.

It would just feel all...wrong.

Everything about this feels wrong.

Does Belinda even know that she's supposed to marry me when she turns eighteen?

I could've asked Grandfather, but I try not to think about these things.

By the time Belinda is eighteen, I'm hoping my Grandfather will be dead and buried and this family legacy is burned to ashes.

Grandfather, McAllister, and I then take our seats. The butler—yes, McAllister has a butler, just like my grandfather—serves shepherd's pie, Irish soda bread, and red wine from a decanter. From a separate decanter, he pours something that looks like apple juice into the wine glass next to Belinda's plate.

This is just unreal.

Then, in what seems really out of place, McAllister takes Belinda's hand. "Shall we say grace?"

Am I supposed to take Belinda's hand?

God, please no.

But she grabs my hand, so what to do? I dart a glance toward McAllister, who takes my grandfather's hand.

This is so very strange.

McAllister says a few words of gratitude for the meal, but

I'm not listening. All I'm thinking about is how wrong this little girl's hand feels in mine.

It feels like a child's hand. Which of course is what it is.

When the prayer is over, Belinda releases my hand, but something feels...

I look down in my palm. Belinda has placed a piece of paper in it.

What's going on?

I discreetly place it in my pocket. I look over at Belinda, hoping to meet her gaze to somehow tell her that yes, I got her message.

But she's still not looking at me.

I won't have a chance to look at the paper until we're done with this godforsaken lunch.

"Dig in," McAllister says. "Dena is an amazing cook."

I draw a breath and place my cloth napkin across my lap, thinking again of the paper in my pocket.

I take a bite of shepherd's pie and bring it to my mouth. Despite the fact that I'm not hungry at all, it is delicious. The whipped potatoes on top of the pie are creamy and flavorful, and the filling is savory and delicious.

I butter a piece of soda bread and bring that to my mouth next.

A little bland, but oddly hearty. I take a sip of water to get it down, and then I try the wine.

It's good. A basic red table wine, Italian, I think. Not overly nuanced, but it pairs perfectly with the shepherd's pie. I would've thought McAllister would pull out all the stops for this lunch, but he's serving us basic red wine.

Which is of course fine with me.

Because God knows I need a fucking drink. The bourbon

didn't quite get me where I need to be to get through this painful ordeal.

Then again, I want my wits about me. Things could go south between my grandfather and McAllister at any time.

"Vinnie," McAllister says, "how's your golf game?"

Oh my God, seriously? We're mobsters. We don't play golf. Do we?

"Nonexistent," I say.

He raises an eyebrow. "We'll have to change that. The best deals are made over golf games, right, Mario?"

Does my grandfather golf? I should know that.

"I don't think golf will be my thing, Declan," I say. "I prefer to do business in an office. Or over a drink."

"We all enjoy that," McAllister says.

Belinda sits next to me, looking at her plate the whole time. She still hasn't made eye contact with any of us that I can see.

She's been trained well. Be a good woman and stay put and shut up.

But she's also been trying to stand out as a piano prodigy.

The poor little girl. She deserves so much more than what she has been born into.

Thank God Savannah didn't suffer this fate.

My own mother did. She was married off at eighteen. Grandfather's only child, and he chose my father for her. I'm sure he had a reason for that, though he doesn't seem to think much of my father anymore.

There's a story there that I don't know. A story I'll need to ferret out. I need to find every skeleton in my grandfather's closet if I'm going to take him down.

We finish our lunch with small talk among the three of us grown-ups while Belinda continues to be silent.

Our plates are clear, and dessert arrives. Simple vanilla ice cream with caramel sauce.

"Belinda's favorite again," McAllister announces. "The caramel sauce is homemade."

"You have excellent taste, Belinda," my grandfather says. "Who needs chocolate when you can have vanilla?"

"Belinda is allergic to chocolate," McAllister says. "So we've learned to really love vanilla in this household." He slowly moves his gaze onto me. "It was Miles's favorite too."

Dead silence.

Miles, who tried to rape Savannah, and he was ready to kill Falcon until my father killed him.

And here we all are, eating shepherd's pie and ice cream, talking as if none of that ever happened. Like we're just all the best fucking friends.

I can't help turning to look at Belinda when her older brother is mentioned.

She's tugging on her lower lip with her teeth. It's the first time I've seen any kind of facial expression from her at all.

He was her big brother.

He may have been a rapist, a criminal, and a genuine piece of shit, but maybe he was nice to her. Who the hell knows?

Everybody has family.

Christ. Puzo had a wife and kids, too. He may have been a mobster piece of shit, but he had people who loved him and depended on him. Maybe his wife knew what he was doing to support their lavish lifestyle. But his kids certainly didn't.

And his nanny, apparently an old friend of Raven's, couldn't have known about his dealings.

I force the thought out of my head. He was a bad man. The world is better off with him gone.

More small talk as we finish our dessert.

Finally, the butler comes in to clear the table.

McAllister rises. "Gentlemen, would you like to join me for a cigar on the veranda?"

A young woman enters. "Miss Belinda, it's time for your afternoon lesson."

Belinda looks up at her father.

He nods slightly at her. "Go ahead, darling."

Belinda rises from her chair, still not making eye contact with any of us. "It was lovely to meet all of you," she says and then follows the young woman—her nanny?—out of the dining room.

Only then, while my grandfather rises and is otherwise engaged talking to McAllister, do I have a chance to pull out the note in my pocket.

My heart stops as I glance at it.

Please help me.

9

RAVEN

Lunch with my mother turns out to be more difficult than I anticipated.

The stares.

People don't mean to be rude. They're just curious. They see a woman with no eyebrows and peach fuzz on her head, and they can't help but take a closer look.

They wonder what my story is. Have I been ill? Am I getting better? Will I die soon?

Or maybe they think I'm in a heavy metal band. Or a cult.

"Ignore it," Mom says. "Don't let it bother you."

"Are you kidding?" I roll my eyes. "It's not that it bothers me. I'm so happy to be alive, especially after what happened to..."

"Sweetheart, what happened to the attorney wasn't your fault."

"I know." I sigh, looking over my menu. "I just wish..."

"Wish what, honey?"

Wish I could be honest. Wish I could tell you about the Uber driver and the drone flying over my backyard. Wish I could tell you I'm in love with Vinnie Gallo, and that the thought of never seeing him again...

Nope, can't say any of that.

"I'm fine." I clear my throat. "As fine as I can be, at least. I think I'll have a cheeseburger."

"That sounds great. I'll have the same."

My appetite has been ravenous since I've been recovering. It's like my body is telling me to put back on the weight I lost. Build up those muscles again. Even when my heart is breaking—and on a normal day that would take away my appetite—it hasn't happened.

"And what can I get the two of you today?" Our server stops at the table.

"Cheeseburger," I say. "Medium, with all the fixings."

"You got it. Would you like fries with that?"

"Onion rings, I think."

"Perfect." She makes notes and turns to my mother. "And for you, ma'am?"

"The same. Only fries for me instead of rings. And a diet soda."

"Yes, of course." She turns back to me. "I forgot to get your drink, ma'am."

"Do you have Orange Crush?"

"I'm afraid we don't. We have orange juice."

Bleh.

"Just a diet cola will be fine then. Thanks."

"You ask every time," Mom laughs. "And no restaurant ever has it."

"One might someday." I unfold my napkin and place it in my lap.

Mom rakes her gaze over me slowly. "So how are things

coming over at your house?" she asks. "Are you getting everything set up for you to settle in?"

More than she knows. "Yes, it's coming along great."

A brand-new security system, plus a new bodyguard. But if I tell her about the bodyguard, she'll just worry.

The rest of lunch goes by with a half hour of inane chitchat. No dessert—though I was craving something a little sweet. Mom settles the bill and then we walk over to the movie theater.

Mom scans the walls of movie posters lining the box office area. "Which one were you thinking of seeing, sweetheart?"

"The new Matt Damon one looked pretty good."

Mom wrinkles her nose. "He never did much for me."

I frown. "Did you have something else in mind?"

"No, of course not." Mom squeezes my shoulder. "We'll see whatever you want to see."

We grab our tickets, and Mom raises her eyebrows when I dogleg toward the snack bar.

"You're still hungry?"

I nod. "I'm always hungry, Mom. My body is, anyway. Sometimes I have to force the food through my mouth to give my body the sustenance it longs for."

She smiles. "I suppose that's a good thing." She grabs her wallet and hands me her credit card. "Get whatever you like, angel."

I smile at her. Mom still loves to pretend like I'm twelve years old when we go out and do things like this. As if I don't have millions in my trust fund that can cover the overpriced bucket of popcorn I'm about to purchase.

I end up getting the largest bucket, along with extra

butter, of course. On a whim I also get a bag of M&M's, which I dump unceremoniously into the popcorn. Sweet and salty.

The nice thing about the movie is that I don't have to talk. Mom was chatting all through lunch to distract us both from what happened with Brick. Now the movie can do the chatting for us.

I munch on my popcorn, barely absorbing the plot of the film.

A few hours later, we make the drive back home.

Only to find my father there, along with Falcon and Leif.

"Oh God," I say. "I guess they're not finished yet."

"It's okay." Mom sighs. "I'll deal."

Once we're out of the car, we join them.

Leif is explaining the new system, and when he's done, Dad looks at Falcon.

"I need to speak with you and Leif. Now."

What about? But I don't ask. If Falcon needs to tell me, he will.

Once Falcon and Leif head back to my father's study, Mom gives me a quick hug. "This was a fun day, Raven. A nice escape. We should do it more often."

I force a smile. It's difficult, and not because I didn't enjoy the day with my mother. I did. It's difficult because I'm hiding so much from her, and I hate that.

"I had a great time too, Mom. And yeah, we need to do it a lot. I don't want to lose sight of my family. Never again will I lose sight of what's important."

"I don't think you ever took us for granted," she says.

"I didn't. But when things are going well, you tend to stop remembering to be grateful for what you have. I won't do that anymore. I love you, Mom."

"Even though I've been hovering?"

I laugh. "Especially because of that. Yeah, it's annoying. I won't lie. But I know how much you care. How much you love me. How much my illness affected you and Dad as much as it did me. I'm sorry I put you through that."

"Raven, honey, we know it wasn't your fault."

"I know. But still. Thank you. Thank you for getting me the best care possible. Thank you for hardly ever leaving my side." I squeeze my arms around her. "Just thank you. For everything."

"You never have to thank me for anything, Raven." She breaks out of the embrace and checks her watch. "Heavens, look at the time. I'm still full from that cheeseburger, but I'd better get dinner planned."

I nod and smile.

And then I walk down the hallway toward my father's study. I strain my ears against the door, hoping to catch a word.

10

VINNIE

Please help me.

I discreetly shove the note back in my pocket.

Now what?

Is my grandfather going to join McAllister for a cigar? Because if he does, I'll be obligated to join too. Which perhaps isn't a bad thing. The longer I'm here, the better chance I may have to get to Belinda. To find out why she needs my help.

But on the other hand, how do I do that?

How do I try to get a little girl alone without looking like a *bona fide* creep?

Without *feeling* like a *bona fide* creep?

I know my intentions are honorable, but no one else will.

The fact that I'm promised to this girl makes the whole thing even more disgusting.

Why did she give me this note? Is someone harming her?

She lives here with McAllister. Her mother passed away a few years ago. As far as I know, she and Miles have the same mother, despite their age difference.

There's got to be a story there, but I don't know it.

She has a butler, a housekeeper, and a nanny, so she's not alone here with her father.

But I also know what her father does for a living.

He traffics not only in drugs but in human beings.

God only knows what he's doing to this little girl.

Or it could be something simpler.

Perhaps she knows of our impending nuptials, and she wants my help getting out of it. That help I'd be happy to give her. Of course, I can't tell her that if everything goes according to my plan, neither one of us will be bound into that marriage by the time she's eighteen.

Maybe that's all it is.

But my God, what if it's something horrible?

She's a child.

And she's asking for my help.

I have to help her.

When my grandfather and McAllister rise, I follow suit.

"When's the last time you smoked a Cuban, Vinnie?" McAllister asks.

"Not since I was in Europe," I say.

He grins. "Today's your lucky day. Let's go out on the veranda, shall we?"

"Absolutely." I nod. "But if you'll excuse me, I need to use the restroom first."

"Of course. There's one right off the foyer." He points. "Meet us out back."

I nod. "Looking forward to it." I'd be a moron to think that this entire house isn't surveilled, but I have to take a chance. This little girl's life might be depending on me.

Once my grandfather and McAllister leave the dining

room, I walk out into the foyer as well, where I locate the door leading to the powder room.

I don't actually have to use the facilities, so I head back into the living room where I assume I will find Belinda at the piano.

But she's not there. When her nanny mentioned a lesson, she must have meant a different kind of lesson.

I walk out of the family room and down a hallway lined with doors. This house is huge. About the same size as my grandfather's.

I find one door cracked open, and inside I hear Belinda reciting.

Some type of academic lesson apparently.

I shouldn't interrupt, but how else am I going to find out what's going on with her?

What the hell? I push the door open.

Belinda stops talking, darting her gaze to me. It's the first time she's actually looked me in the eyes since I got here. Seated across from her is the young woman who I thought was her nanny. Perhaps she's more like a teacher.

"Excuse me," I say. "I must've gotten lost."

I look Belinda in the eye, hoping that I'm showing her kindness, showing her that she can talk to me.

"Are you okay, Belinda?" I ask.

She doesn't respond.

The nanny rises and comes toward me. "You shouldn't be in here."

Do I trust the nanny? She's a young woman—no more than twenty-five or twenty-six years old. I look again to Belinda, and she gives me a slight nod.

I take it at face value. I pull the note out of my pocket and show it to the nanny.

She nods, picks up her purse, pulls out a card, and hands it to me.

"Now go," she whispers right into my ear. "Quickly, before they miss you."

Only then do I see the camera mounted at the top of the door. By sheer luck I managed to stay out of its sight. But no doubt they heard the sounds I made.

I'll stick with my story of getting lost. Even though McAllister told me point-blank the bathroom was off the foyer. Maybe he'll believe I'm just that stupid.

I'll have to trust the nanny to take care of it. Maybe there isn't a sound system. Maybe only a camera. I don't know.

I can't worry about it now.

I'm in too deep.

When a child asks me for help, I have to help her.

I should've been around to help Mikey and Savannah. Maybe helping Belinda will help me make up for that, help me feel less guilt.

She looks fine and healthy. Not a mark on her. But not all abuse leaves marks. And the most private parts of her are covered.

I don't dare look at the card the nanny gave me. I'll deal with that alone. It may be a phone number, a meeting place, only a name. I don't know.

At the moment I need to get back out to the deck and smoke a Cuban with two men I detest.

At least a delicious Cuban will make it bearable.

Grandfather and McAllister are already lit up and nursing brandies when I appear outside.

"Vinnie," McAllister says, "sit down right here. I picked out a robust Cohiba for you. Already cut."

"Obliged," I say as I take a seat.

I take the lighter he offers and light the cigar, inhaling a bit of the smoke. Cubans are great, no lie about that. There's nothing like it. This one has a Sumatra wrapper, and it tastes of smoky caramel.

"Brandy?" McAllister asks.

"No, thank you. A lot of work to do when I get back to the office."

I've already had wine and a drink before lunch. But I'd like for Grandfather and McAllister to keep drinking. *In vino veritas* and all.

So I change my mind. "On second thought, I will have a drink."

"That's the ticket, Vinnie." McAllister pours me a brandy.

I take it, nodding my thanks, and take a small sip.

Except I don't actually take a sip. I feign it. Let them think I'm drinking. That way they might be a little more loose-tongued.

"So Vinnie, my boy," McAllister says. "What do you think of my lovely Belinda?"

Oh, God help me. He wants me to assess a child.

"She's very pretty and quite talented," I say.

Right. That didn't make me sound creepy at all.

"She is that," Grandfather agrees. "She looks a lot like her late mother, may she rest in peace."

"Yes," McAllister says. "Sienna was a lovely woman. I miss her every day." He takes a puff from his cigar. "Already my Belinda is blossoming into a woman." He elbows me. "She'll be ready for you soon, son."

A fresh wave of nausea envelops my throat, and I have to stop myself from coughing from the cigar smoke.

She's a little girl. No evidence of blossoming whatsoever. At least not from what I can see.

Of course, he is her father. He's watched her grow up. And even if he hasn't, he's probably received reports from her doctors about how she's developing.

God, I hope that's the case.

"You all right there, Gallo?" McAllister asks.

I swallow. "Yeah, just inhaled a bit by mistake."

McAllister exchanges a look with my grandfather, but then they continue to prattle on.

I nod, murmur agreement every now and then as the two of them talk as if they've been friends their whole lives. Forget the fact that my father just killed his son.

It's like that never happened. Like they're old friends, comrades. And he's giving his daughter to me.

Hell, if I threatened to take her now, he'd probably allow it.

Maybe that's what I should do. She obviously wants my help. What better way to help her than to get her out of this damned house?

I will not marry an eleven-year-old. It wouldn't be legal anyway, even though I know it's done. And of course I would never touch her. Even if it comes to the forced marriage when she's eighteen, I still won't touch her. But I plan to have taken the family down before then.

I'll have to think of another way to get her out of here.

"I believe she'll make a lovely wife for you, Vincent," Grandfather says.

They both look to me.

Seriously? They want me to comment on what a good wife a little girl is going to make me?

What do I say without sounding horrific?

"I'm sure she will mature into a beautiful woman," I say.

There, that kept the creep factor to a minimum. But it didn't eliminate it altogether.

"She certainly will." McAllister swirls his brandy around his glass.

"Tell me," I say. "What are your plans for her musical talent? Where could that lead?"

"Nowhere, really," McAllister says. "She'll be marrying you when she turns eighteen. But I'm sure she'll play for you whenever you'd like to hear it. Imagine, having your own concert pianist in your home." He closes his eyes. "I will miss that. Hearing Belinda play is one of the most wonderful things in my life."

"Don't you feel she should have collegiate training? She could be something great," I say.

"You could send her to a school nearby," Grandfather says. "What you do for her once she's your property is up to you."

I cock my head at him. I really just heard that. He referred to a woman as property. That must be what he thought of my grandmother. What he thinks of my mother. What he thought of Savannah, and why he was willing to give her to Miles McAllister.

I feel sick.

The shepherd's pie and ice cream are sitting in my stomach like a lump, and they could come traveling up at any moment.

For a brief time I regret coming back to the States.

But then I remember Savannah. What she would be going through if I hadn't returned.

What my father would be going through.

No, this is *my* blood right. *My* legacy. And I plan to burn it to the ground.

11

RAVEN

Despite straining my ears, all I hear are muffled voices.

Surely they're just talking about the new system, how it works and such. What else would they be discussing?

Our father is a kind man, but he's also a stern man. There's a reason why the five of us are so strong. We got that nurturing kind of love from our mother, but from our father? He showed his love in a different way.

He taught us strength, determination, confidence. He taught us to stand on our own two feet, learn the value of a dollar and a hard day's work. We were born rich, but we never had silver spoons in our mouths. Our father saw to that.

He learned from his father, Brick Bellamy, who made this ranch what it is today. The ranch does well. Better than most, but our true money comes from our grandmother, the Cooper Steel heiress.

But she never spoiled my father. My grandfather wouldn't

have it, and my father never spoiled us. Sure, we have trust funds, but we couldn't touch them until we turned twenty-one.

I'll use a large chunk of mine to fund my nonprofit. Help others. To help those in my shoes who don't have the resources that I was so lucky to have.

A moment later I jerk backward as the door opens, and my father stands there.

"Raven? What exactly are you doing?"

"Just heading to the library," I lie.

I try to meet Falcon's gaze through the door to the study, but he seems to be looking beyond me.

To complete my ruse, I walk through the door next to the study. I don't want a book. I don't feel like reading. All I can think about is what a mess all of this is.

A second later, I correct my thinking. I'm alive. Every day is a gift. Every obstacle is a gift. I'm going to get through this. My family will get through this.

And Vinnie...

Vinnie, who sneaked out of my bed in the middle of the night and left no communication at all. Vinnie, who I haven't heard from since then.

Vinnie...who I love.

How do you fall in love so quickly? Because there's no doubt in my mind that it *is* love. Something I've never felt before, and I've had plenty of boyfriends. One or two serious relationships even.

Never did I consider a life with any of those men.

But Vinnie? Despite what he does for a living, if he asked, I'd have him in a heartbeat.

I grab a book off the shelf. I don't even bother looking at

the title, and when I leave the library, I look for Falcon and Leif. I walk down the hallway, and I find them still talking to my father, but in the kitchen this time.

I walk past them to the family room where I sit down with the book.

I need to speak to Falcon alone. A man is dead.

What the hell is this screwed-up world I'm living in?

I should get past Vinnie. He's not good for me. He told me as much.

But my God…

He invades my every thought. Every single thought.

I need to see him. At least talk to him. Find out why he left so abruptly. Tell him what happened to Brick Latham.

He hasn't answered, but maybe he'll answer if I use the burner phone Falcon gave me.

I punch in the number.

No answer. It eventually goes to voicemail.

You've reached Vincent Gallo Junior. I apologize that I can't take your call at the moment. Please leave a detailed message and I'll return your call as soon as I get the chance.

That's it, in his beautiful deep monotone voice.

Nothing like how it sounded when he was looking in my eyes, telling me how beautiful I am.

Will he return the call this time?

I open the book that I pulled off the library shelf. Then I laugh out loud. *The Godfather* by Mario Puzo.

I grabbed a fucking Mafia book.

Who says the universe doesn't have a sense of humor?

12

VINNIE

Two hours later I'm back in my office. I grab a burner phone, leave the office, and then leave the building. I'm on the streets of downtown Austin when I call the number the nanny left on the card.

It was just a number. No name. Nothing else.

"Hello?"

"Yes, hello. You gave me this number?"

"I'm afraid I don't know what you're talking about, sir. Are you trying to reach Freddie's dry-cleaning? Because I get my number mistaken for theirs a lot."

Is this some kind of message? I don't know, but I decide to play long. "Yes, I am. My apologies. Looks like I transposed a few numbers. So sorry for the bother."

"Not at all. I'm used to it. Have a good day, sir. I'm sure you'll be able to get in touch with them soon."

The call ends with a click.

Then I wait.

Five minutes go by. Then ten. Just as it's coming up on

fifteen minutes, my phone buzzes with a number I don't recognize.

"Yes?" I say into the phone.

"Vincent Gallo?"

"Freddie's dry-cleaning?" I say.

"Yes. My name is Natalie. I'm on a burner phone while I'm out running errands at the grocery store. You got me at a good time. I was able to leave the house."

"You're Belinda's nanny?"

"Yes. More like a governess. I take care of her, and I see to her lessons."

"How do I know you can be trusted?" I ask.

"How do I know *you* can be?" she says back.

I frown. "Seems we're at an impasse then."

"I only want to protect Belinda."

"Then we have something in common."

"If you truly intend to marry her, Mr. Gallo, there's something you should know."

How much can I truly say to this woman? I don't intend to marry that child, but do I need to act like I do?

"Go on," I say.

"She's special. I'm not just talking about the fact that she's a musical prodigy, which she is. Her IQ is excellent, nearing genius level, and her father..."

I already know where this is going. After what my grandfather did to me, I don't labor under any delusion that these people are above harming children. After all, the McAllisters *deal* in children. And he was acting pretty lecherous when he was talking about her over our cigars.

"And her father what?" I say, my voice low and dark.

"He... He harms her."

I knew it was coming. Even so, my stomach sinks like I just swallowed an anvil.

"I... I had a feeling that was the case. Why else would she have asked me for help?"

Her voice cracks as she continues. "She doesn't tell me a lot, Mr. Gallo. She's scared. So very frightened. I tell her she can trust me, but she's still not completely honest with me."

"Why did she feel she could trust *me*? She's the one who gave me that note."

"That was my idea," Natalie says. "I thought... If you were going to be the one who would eventually marry her, perhaps you would be interested in helping her."

"I'm very interested in helping her. But I'm not sure what I can do."

"Can you get her out of the house?"

"You realize that would mean you're out of a job, Natalie."

She sighs. "I don't care about that. I've been with Belinda for two years now, and I've grown to love her as if she were my own. I can't stand the pain that she's in. I can't stand how he trots her out as a showpiece when people come over, as he did with you and your grandfather today. She hates that. But what can she do?"

"I wish I could help."

"He's going to break her, Mr. Gallo. He's going to take that beautiful and talented little girl and strip her of everything."

"But why would he do that if—"

I stop abruptly. That's exactly why he would do it. Revenge. He wants to leave me a shell of a human being for a wife. Even at the cost of his own daughter's mental health.

These bastards truly think of women and girls as chattel and nothing more. Pawns in the big boys' games with each other. They don't see them as human at all, not even when they're defenseless children with no means of fighting for themselves. It's disgusting. Just the thought of it sends a wave of anger through my entire body.

I have to stop this.

"Let me think about this, Natalie. You can reach me on this burner phone when you need to. I'll see what I can do, but I can't make any promises."

"Please, Mr. Gallo. If you care anything at all about this little girl..."

"I don't even *know* this little girl, Natalie. But I won't sit around while any child is harmed. I just have to figure out the best way to go about this."

"Please don't tell Mr. McAllister that I reached out to you. I don't regret it. I would do anything for Belinda." She sucks in a breath. "But if he finds out..."

"I know. Trust me, this will stay between the two of us."

I'm tempted to tell her everything. That Belinda and I will never be married, and that the Bianchis and the McAllisters will be out of business as soon as I can make it happen.

But I can't.

I can't tell anyone that.

Not until it's over.

"All right. Thank you, Mr. Gallo. I need to get back to the house. And I still have to stop at the store so I have some groceries to show for my trip."

"I understand. Reach out on the burner whenever you need to. And I'll be in touch." I shove the burner back in my pocket and pull out my regular smartphone.

I have a missed call. From a number I don't recognize.

Dare I call it back on this phone?

I pull out my burner again and tap in the number.

"Hello?"

God, that sweet voice. It's Raven. Raven tried to call me. I already had two missed calls from her regular number.

"Hi, Raven," I say.

"Oh my God, Vinnie." She lowers her voice. "How are you? Are you okay?"

So very Raven. The first thing she thinks of is me. How *I'm* doing. When I'm the one who left her alone in her bed in the middle of the night and then proceeded to screen her calls all day.

I don't deserve this woman. No one does.

"I'm fine. More importantly, how are *you*?"

"So much is going on, Vinnie. I mean, physically I'm fine, but..."

"But what?" I ask.

"That lawyer. The one who asked me out."

"Right. What about him?"

She pauses. "You really don't know?"

My heart begins to accelerate, and I'm not sure why. "I have no idea what you're talking about, Raven."

"You mean it's not all over the news?"

"What the hell are you talking about? What happened?"

"He must not have gotten my text in time. You know, my text breaking the date. So he showed up at our house. But my parents were out for the evening and..."

Her voice is sad, fearful.

"Baby, what happened?" I say, my voice lowering an octave.

"Someone...*killed* him, Vinnie."

My stomach drops out from under me. This couldn't possibly be the work of my—

"Someone killed him, and then got into our house, and..." She starts crying.

"For the love of God, Raven. What the hell happened?"

"My mother found him in my bed. In my bed in her house. His throat was slit, Vinnie. There was a note attached to the body."

This can't mean anything good. "What did the note say, Raven?"

"It didn't make any sense."

I have a horrible feeling it'll make sense to me, but I don't say that.

"What did it say?" I grit out.

"It's said, 'your move, Cobra.'"

My blood runs cold.

My fucking grandfather. But why would he leave such a note when he's the cobra?

Except he's the *king* cobra.

"Vinnie?"

I can't respond to her yet. I'm too damned angry.

"Vinnie, are you there?"

"I'm here."

"Do you know what the note means?"

Do I tell her I do? She'll only worry about me. It's enough that I'm worried about her.

"No. I'm sorry. I don't."

"You think it has something to do with..."

"Don't say anything else, Raven. Please."

She lets out another sob. "He was helping me. The attorney. He was helping me set up my nonprofit. It's because of me that—"

"Don't you dare go there," I tell her. "Don't you dare take the blame for any of this."

"Vinnie... Why did you..."

I swallow. I try to find the right words. The last thing I want to do is hurt this woman. This beautiful, wonderful woman who I love more than my life.

"It's better this way," I say. "I love you, Raven. But trust me. It's better this way."

"No. I don't accept that. If you love me—"

"I do. Don't ever question that. It's because I love you that I've chosen to stay away from you. I should've never let it go as far as it did."

"So you regret it then?"

Oh, she's jabbed a stake into my heart. "Regret it? Being with you? Of course not. I regret everything else. Regret having to leave you. Because if I don't, you'll only be in more danger."

"Falcon and Leif found surveillance equipment in my home."

"That doesn't surprise me. Why do you think I insisted that we go outside to talk on Friday?"

"I didn't want to believe it."

"Believe everything I tell you about what my family is capable of, Raven. I'm sorry you had to see so much of it. That's why I need to stay away from you. So it doesn't touch you again."

"Can you do it?"

"What? Stay away from you?"

She pauses. "Yes."

God, that voice. So much emotion in that one little word. *Yes*. She's clawing at my heart, and how I want to give in. How I want to drive over to her right now, take her away, and keep driving. To Mexico. To Canada. Somewhere where we're both away from all of this. Where it can't touch us anymore. Where all we have to do is love each other.

But that leaves my sister vulnerable. My mother and father as well. And that poor little girl, Belinda.

I can't in good conscience leave them to fend for themselves just for my own happiness.

And there's no guarantee my bastard of a grandfather wouldn't find us anyway. He knows I'm a flight risk, and he's had his eyes on me like a hawk ever since I returned.

So the correct choice is clear.

"I have to," I say. "There is no choice, Raven, if I want to keep you safe. And I want that more than anything in the world."

"So you want to keep me safe more than you want to be with me?"

I rub at my forehead. She's not making this easy on me.

"If I keep you safe now, perhaps we can be together sometime in the future. But being with you now will only put you in danger. I can't have that. I couldn't live with myself. You're everything to me, Raven Bellamy. Every fucking thing. I didn't ask for this. Neither did you. No one could've predicted it. I sure as hell couldn't have. But my heart beats for you, Raven. Every fucking beat. Despite that, I *can* give you up. As much as it hurts me, tears out my own fucking heart, I can give you up to ensure your safety."

"Vinnie..."

"Please. Don't fight me on this. If something were to

happen to you, I wouldn't be able to go on. I wouldn't be able to do what I came back to do. It must be done, Raven. Please believe me. It must be done."

A slight whimper comes through the phone.

God, this is killing me.

"Please don't make it harder than it has to be, Raven. Please…"

The phone call ends with a soft click.

I'm sitting on a bench on a downtown Austin Street.

What I want to do is look to the heavens and scream. Curl my fists and release all the angst from my body into the stratosphere. Why? Why now? Why now did I find the love of my life, only to have to let her go?

The unfairness of it all.

But I have to be stronger. Raven needs her strength for other things. So I need to stay away from her. This is on me. On my shoulders, and I can't let her down.

I draw in a deep breath, rise, and walk back to the office building owned by my grandfather's coffee import company.

This is my life now.

It's become volatile. So volatile. I've killed a man, and now my future bride is being harmed by her father and she has reached out to me for help.

And they know about Raven.

They know about my Achilles' heel.

Which is why I have to stay far away from her.

13

RAVEN

I allow myself five minutes to cry. I freaking bawl my eyes out to the point where seven tissues are now soggy clumps on the bed in one of my parents' guestrooms.

But I gulp back the last tear.

On my burner phone, I call Savannah.

"Hello?"

"Hey, Savannah. It's Raven."

"Ray, are you okay? Is Falcon still over there?"

"Last I checked, yeah. I think they're about done here."

"Okay. But are you sure *you're* all right? You sound kind of...congested."

"I'm fine. But I need a favor."

"Of course. Anything."

"I need the address of your parents' house in Austin."

"Why?"

"I need to see Vinnie, Savannah. I need to see your brother."

"Oh my God, is he all right?"

"Yes, he's fine. I just spoke to him." I wipe my eyes, sniff a few times. "But Savannah..."

"What, Raven? What's going on?"

"Falcon will tell you anyway when he gets home. I'm in love with Vinnie, Savannah. I've fallen in love with your brother."

She doesn't say anything for what seems like an eternity.

Until finally I speak. "Savannah? You there?"

"I'm here," she squeaks. "So many emotions are going through me right now. I'm thrilled for you and Vinnie, of course. But..."

"Believe me, I know all the buts. He's already told me that being with him will put me in danger."

"Raven, you have to know that you mean everything to Falcon. Please... I don't want you in danger either."

I wipe a tear from my cheek, willing my voice to remain steady. "But I've fallen in love."

"Does my brother feel the same way?"

"Yes. He does. At least he says he does. It all seems so unreal, Savannah. How do you fall in love in such a short time?"

"It was pretty quick for Falcon and me," she says. "Though probably not quite as quick as for you and Vinnie." She chuckles lightly. "I guess when you know, you know."

"Exactly."

"But Raven. Your family almost lost you. If something were to happen to you... I don't know if they could survive it."

I look out the window of the guestroom. "What is survival anyway, though? Right now I'm surviving. I'm recovering and I'm so happy to be alive. But without Vinnie... Don't get me wrong. I've learned to appreciate everything so much more.

The color of the sky, the smell of the cut grass. The beauty and aroma of the wildflowers. But with Vinnie… Everything is even more vibrant. How do you turn your back on that?"

She pauses again.

Until finally, "I wish I had an answer for you. Truly I do. I've been in your situation. I forced myself to turn my back on Falcon when I went willingly with Miles. And I did it for Falcon. To keep him safe. It was the hardest thing I've ever done."

"And didn't Falcon hate that you did that?"

She sighs. "He did. But I think after a while he understood why I chose to do what I did. Just as you will understand Vinnie's choice."

"So you're saying sometimes there isn't a choice. You have to give up your love. You want me to give him up."

She sniffles through the phone. "Believe me, Raven, none of this is what I want. And I was lucky because Falcon and I got to be together eventually. But look at the havoc we wreaked, the fallout left in our wake. Miles is gone. He was a terrible man, but no matter how you slice it, a man is dead. And my father—who I do care about because he's a good man at heart—will spend the rest of his life in prison. My mother's life will never be the same. And neither will Vinnie's."

I sigh. "Perhaps you're stronger than I am. Perhaps you were able to give up your great love. Maybe you knew, somewhere deep down, that it would work out eventually. But I don't see how I can do it, Savannah. I made a commitment when my recovery from cancer was imminent. I made a commitment to live each day to the fullest. To be the happiest

I could be. He makes me happy, Savannah. I'd rather have one day with him than a lifetime without him."

She doesn't reply.

"I suppose that makes me sound selfish," I continue. "In a way it is. When you've looked your life in the eye, and you've accepted the fact that it may be over, you let go of that fear. And of course that doesn't mean that I'm not incredibly grateful to be alive. I am. And if Vinnie and I can't be together, I will deal with that. I won't let it ruin my life. But I have to try, Savannah. I have to try to be with the love of my life."

And again, nothing.

I like my sister-in-law. I love her, even. But I don't think she understands. Yes, she was willing to give up her great love. To do her duty to her family to ensure the safety of the man she loves.

But at the end of the day, she got to be with her love. He came for *her*.

This time it seems the decision is mine to make.

Finally, her voice comes through the other end of the phone. "Raven," she says, "I've been in fear for my life as well. When those two men came to Falcon's house to grab me. They had guns trained on Falcon, and everything was up to me..."

"I know. I'm not trying to belittle what you've been through. What you and Falcon have both been through. And I respect the hell out of you, Savannah. Your strength and fortitude. But I'm not you. And I'm not willing to give your brother up."

"Raven... I'm sure he's told you to stay away."

"He has."

"And you want to defy his wishes?"

Her question makes me think.

I've let the selfishness grab hold of me, and perhaps I shouldn't have.

"I'm going to give you the address," she says. "You'd be able to get it from Falcon anyway because he would never deny you anything. But Raven, I'm begging you. Please. If not for your own sake, then for Falcon's. Stay out of danger. Come back to us."

She rattles off the address and I program it into the burner phone.

It's a two-hour drive, which is far longer than my doctor cleared me for.

But I'm going to do it anyway.

If I leave now, by the time I get there, it will be about dinnertime.

"You should know," Savannah says, "that the place is a fortress. You need a code to get through the gate. Otherwise you'll have to call the butler on the intercom."

"What's the code?"

No reply.

"Savannah, please. I'm going one way or the other. You can make it difficult for me or easy for me. The fewer people who know I'm going, the better for me and for Vinnie. So if I can get right through..."

"Fine." She gives me the code. "Please. Falcon is going to give me holy living hell for this. Please stay safe, Raven."

"I'm going to your mother's home. If it's a fortress as you say, I'll be safer there than I am in my own place."

Again, silence.

Until— "I love you, Raven. Falcon loves you. And I'm sure Vinnie does as well. So please, for all of us, make it back here."

14

VINNIE

I make it home to Mom's house by six p.m. I spent the remainder of the day ruminating over Raven—asking her to stay away from me, and regretting it.

In between that, I thought about Belinda and how I could help her.

Would her father allow me to marry her now? It's disgusting to even think about, and is it even allowed with parental consent?

I wouldn't touch her, of course. She would simply live in my home with Mom and me in her own room. I would treat her like a daughter.

The idea sickens me, but how else can I help her?

Perhaps I don't have to marry her to bring her to my home. Aren't there some cultures where the intended lives in the husband's home until she comes of age?

Oh hell, who knows? And who cares? None of this is possible.

As much as I want to help the girl, I just can't.

She should be playing piano, exploring her musical

talent, going to competitions, getting scholarships—not being abused by her father and being groomed to be a Mafia wife.

How can I help her?

"Vinnie, what's troubling you?" My mother asks as I sit down next to her for dinner.

It's chicken parmesan with a side of spaghetti. One of my favorites, next to lasagna. But I'm not at all hungry.

And I'm not amused by my mother's question.

"What *isn't* troubling me?" I retort. "You know the life we're leading. It's fucked up, Mom."

She wrinkles her nose. "You know I don't like that language."

I slam my fork down on the table. "I don't like this *life* I'm living. This is my home now, until I build my own. And I'm the head of this home. I'll speak the way I want to."

My mother looks down at her lap.

What the hell is wrong with me?

"I'm sorry," I mumble.

"You've been spending too much time with your grandfather."

I swallow. "It's not like I have a choice in the matter, Mom. If I'd stayed in the beginning, Mikey would still be alive, and Savannah would never have been in the situation of having to marry Miles McAllister. Dad wouldn't be in jail."

She shakes her head curtly. "Don't blame yourself, Vinnie. I don't blame you."

"No, you blame Savannah. Which makes no sense at all."

"I love Savannah," Mom says. "I adore her. But she never knew her place."

"She knows her place just fine. She's a woman of the

twenty-first century. But this family is still living in Victorian times."

"It's just the way it is, Vinnie." She sighs, gazing toward the window. "I was barely eighteen when I was married off to your father. We grew to love each other, but we could've just as easily grown to hate each other."

"I need to talk to you about something," I say. "About Belinda—"

The doorbell rings. "Who could that be?" Mom asks.

The butler answers the door, and a few moments later, he interrupts our dinner. "Pardon me, Mr. Gallo, Mrs. Gallo. There's a young lady here to see you, Mr. Gallo. She says her name is Raven Bellamy."

Just the mention of her name and my heart speeds up.

What is she doing here? How did she even *get* here? She's not supposed to be driving for more than twenty minutes.

Of course, after that Uber fiasco, she probably wouldn't trust a rideshare.

I rise. "Excuse me, Mom."

"She's Falcon's sister," Mom says. "What's she doing here?"

"I'll find out."

"Invite her to join us for dinner," Mom says.

"I'll see."

I walk out of the kitchen dining area to the foyer where Raven stands underneath the grand crystal chandelier.

She's wearing simple jeans, flip-flops, and a white T-shirt. Her cheeks are rosy, her lips pink. She looks beautiful, and both my heart and my dick react.

She gives me a tentative smile. "Hello, Vinnie."

I can't help myself. I walk toward her and take her into my

arms, planting a chaste kiss on her lips before I simply hold her.

But just as quickly, I pull back, meet her gaze. "What are you doing here? I told you today that I can't—"

She places two fingers over my lips. "I know what you said. If you can look me in the eye and tell me to go away, I will. But I won't accept it through a phone call. You have to look me in the eye. Tell me you don't want to be with me."

"Whether or not I want to be with you is irrelevant," I say, "and you know it, Raven. I can't keep you safe, and that kills me."

She widens her eyes. "I believe you *can* keep me safe. I believe I can keep *you* safe. Safe in the bubble of our love."

I let out a breath of air. "If only it were that simple."

"Maybe it can be. Maybe it can't. But I can tell you one thing." She wraps her arms around my waist and gives me a squeeze. "I didn't go through hell and survive cancer just to have the greatest love of my life taken away from me right as our relationship is beginning to blossom. It's not fair. To either of us."

I grab her hand and lead her into the living room, where I gesture her to sit down on the couch. I sit next to her.

"Raven," I say, "you don't know anything about me."

"I know how you make me feel." She pounds a fist against her heart. "That's all I need to know."

Maybe I just need to tell her. Tell her that I'm responsible for not one but two deaths now. One that I took in Eastern Europe in self-defense and was lucky enough to get away with, and one that I took mere days ago. The night she and I were together. The night I left her.

If she knows I'm a killer, maybe she'll leave.

But I can't bring myself to tell her.

I can't lose her love. Maybe we can't be together, but at least I know in my heart that this amazing woman loves me.

I need that. I need that knowledge to get through what's coming.

"So are you going to tell me then?" she asks.

I raise an eyebrow. "What? Tell you to your face that we can't be together?"

She crosses her arms. "Yes. That's what I need you to do."

I open my mouth, but then my mother's voice interrupts us.

"Are you going to invite your friend to join us for dinner?"

Raven pops up off the couch. "You must be Mrs. Gallo. I'm Raven, Falcon's sister. I'd love to join you for dinner."

My mother smiles at her warmly. "It's lovely to finally meet you. Do you like chicken parmesan?"

"I love it."

Raven follows my mother into the kitchen to the large table where we eat. We don't use the formal dining room since it's just the two of us.

My mom gestures Raven to sit on my other side. "Phyllis, could you please set another plate?"

"Right away, ma'am."

Once Raven's place is set, my mother herself takes the plate and dishes up a generous portion of chicken parmesan and spaghetti marinara. "I hope you're hungry," she says. "Phyllis always makes enough to feed an army."

Raven eyes the food and grins. "Yes, I am hungry. Thank you."

Why isn't my mother asking Raven what she's doing here? This is all so surreal.

Mother spears a piece of chicken with her fork. "How are your parents doing?"

Raven pauses mid-chew, eyeing me. She's wondering if she should tell my mother about what happened to that lawyer at their house. I subtly shake my head.

She swallows. "They're doing well."

Mom nods. "And your brother?"

I can't help noticing that she doesn't ask about my sister. Her daughter.

"Falcon is great. He and Savannah are fixing up their house quite nicely."

"That's lovely." Mom shifts her gaze to the top of Raven's head. "And how about *you*, dear? How is your recovery going?"

Raven smiles. "Never better. My appetite came back something fierce after the bone marrow transplant. It's been so *great* being able to enjoy the taste of food again. The taste of *life* again."

God, she's something. I remember when we were with Falcon and Savannah, how serene she looked as she was eating the ice cream and raspberries Savannah made. How much she savored every bite.

She's doing the same with the chicken. I can see her taking in every texture. The gooey cheese, the crunchy breading, the moist chicken.

Good God, I'm fucked.

"I'm so glad to hear that," Mom replies to Raven. "Our family has been praying for you."

I nearly choke on my bite of chicken. Maybe Mom has been praying for Raven. There'd be no way of knowing. But it was only a few days ago I was convincing my own goddamned Grandfather not to take a hit out on this woman. I doubt she's been in *his* prayers.

But Mom doesn't know about any of that. And neither does Raven. So I'll keep my mouth shut. My mother continues to pepper Raven with small talk as we finish our dinner. Raven answers each question candidly between bites of food, letting her gorgeous personality slip in every time she utters a word. Mom listens with bright eyes.

The two of them are chatting as if they've known each other forever.

For a moment, I allow myself to imagine that my life is different. That Raven is my girlfriend and I brought her home to meet my mother, and they're getting along famously—which they are.

And that later tonight, perhaps I'm planning to propose to Raven. With a large diamond ring in my pocket.

That I have my mother's approval.

And that the woman I love will be mine forever.

But reality nudges its head back in. Raven and I are not boyfriend and girlfriend. And I'm not proposing to her later tonight. No.

I'm promised to an eleven-year-old girl—an eleven-year-old girl who is being abused and has asked me for help.

I force myself to finish my dinner, and then I sit with an empty plate while Mom and Raven are still chatting as if everything's fine.

But everything's not fine. I've killed two men. My father's in prison for killing another—and God only knows how many more he's killed and gotten away with it. And I'm sure that number pales in comparison to my grandfather's body count.

And Raven… Raven has been thrown into this. Her attorney is dead because of it.

I clear my throat. "Would you ladies excuse me please?"

"Vinnie," Mom says, "don't be rude."

I tap my right pants pocket. "Sorry. I have to make a phone call and it can't wait."

Mom frowns. "All right, but come back quickly. Phyllis made tiramisu for dessert."

I don't actually have to make a phone call. I just need to leave the kitchen for a moment. I need to gather my wits, figure out how best to deal with the situation. Raven is here, and all I can think about is getting her up into my bedroom.

I don't even care that my mother is here in the house.

Of course, there's always the guesthouse. The guesthouse, which is always fully furnished, complete with a pool and hot tub.

Perhaps I should be living there anyway. I just don't want to leave Mom alone. Especially since my grandfather has made it clear that every female member of his family—his daughter included—is an expendable pawn in his game.

But my mind still keeps dwelling on that guesthouse…

Raven and I could be alone there. We could make all the noise we want. I could fuck her into the wee hours of the morning.

But would that change anything?

No. Not a damned thing. It would only make it more difficult to let her go again.

She's made it clear that she's not going to go easily or willingly.

So I'm going to have to demand it. I'm going to have to hurt her.

God, the thought of it…

I draw a breath as I go back to the kitchen. Mom and Raven have cleaned their plates, and Phyllis is setting out the dessert.

"Raven," I say, "may I have a word?"

"We're just about to start dessert, Vinnie." Raven grabs a small plate from Phyllis. "I believe I've told you before that I *never* turn down dessert. I will never turn down dessert again."

Yes, she did say that.

I plunk back into my chair and take a spoonful of the tiramisu that Phyllis placed in front of me.

I'm not a big fan of tiramisu, but it's my mother's favorite.

Dessert drags on. It doesn't help that my mother keeps asking Raven questions, forcing her to slow down her eating. I gobble mine up pretty quickly, leaving a trail of cocoa powder all over the table in my wake. But Raven takes her sweet-ass time. It's like she knows that this might very well be the last time we'll share a meal together.

Once my mother and Raven are both done, and Raven—thank God—says no to coffee, I rise. "Raven, can I speak with you outside?"

"Of course." She smiles at my mom. "Mrs. Gallo, thank you for the lovely dinner. Everything was delicious. It was so wonderful to meet you."

My mom smiles and gives Raven a hug. "It was a joy to meet you as well."

Finally, I escort Raven toward the French doors that lead out to the large redwood deck. The guesthouse stands in the distance, and I lead Raven toward it.

She glances around and scratches the side of her head. "Where are we going?"

"This is the guesthouse." I walk her to the front door. "You and I are going to go in, and I'm going to fuck you."

Her eyes widen. "But I thought—"

I look away from her. "You thought what, Raven? That you would show up here and nothing would happen? That's bullshit. You came here for this. We both want it. And we're going to have it."

Raven swallows. "Vinnie, I—"

I stop walking, grab her shoulders, and force her to face me. "You knew how this was going to end up as well as I did. You knew it when you came here."

"But I didn't." She wriggles out of my grasp. "You live with your mother. I just wanted to see you. I wanted you to say it to my face, Vinnie."

"Say what to your face?"

She looks down. "That you don't love me. That you don't want to be with me."

I grit my teeth. "You know that isn't true. It's *because* I want to be with you that I can't be. Not until this business with my family is taken care of."

She keeps her gaze down, kicking at a pebble. "Then maybe it's best that we don't sleep together tonight. Best to"—she looks up at me with those soulful doe eyes—"make a clean cut."

"I call bullshit." I grab her hands. "You want me to fuck you, Raven. And I want to fuck you just as badly. Probably more badly."

"Vinnie..."

"I'm done talking, Raven." I pull her into my arms,

carrying her like a child. She's no heavier than a feather in my arms, and I walk the rest of the way to the guesthouse.

I push in the code, disarming the security system to the guesthouse, and open the door.

The guesthouse is nearly as lavish as the main house, though it's quite a bit smaller. A large living and dining room, a smaller kitchen and family area, and three bedrooms round out the one-story home.

With Raven still in my arms, I head down the hallway toward the master bedroom.

I open the door and look her in the eyes.

"Here's your one chance, Raven. You can walk away now. Walk away and don't come back. If you really want that clean cut, now's your chance. Because if you don't? I'm going to fuck you. I'm going to fuck you in this bed. I'm going to fuck you hard. It's not going to be gentle. It's not going to be nice. I'm going to take out all the frustrations of the last couple days on your body, Raven. Are you ready for that? Are you up for it?"

She swallows. "I can take anything you dish out, Vinnie."

"You sure about that?" I narrow my gaze. "Because I can't tell you what the last couple days have been like for me."

She raises a trembling arm, cups my cheek. "You can. You can tell me anything."

I look away, gaze out the window. "If only that were true..."

"But you *can*, Vinnie." She returns her hand to my face and forces me to look at her. "I want you to. I want to help you. Let me be your strength, Vinnie. And I'll let you be mine."

I sigh and stand her on her own feet. "I wish I had strength left to give you, Raven. I'm doing everything I can to keep my own fucking head above water right now with my family. Things have gotten volatile. More volatile than you can even imagine."

"You think I can't imagine volatile?" She crosses her arms. "My attorney had his throat slit while I was with you. I found surveillance equipment in my home—my *home*. Maybe those two things are related to you and maybe they're not. But I'll tell you what *doesn't* have anything to do with you. Falcon spent eight years in prison. There's a drug lord buried under my father's old barn. You want to talk about volatile? My whole family is volatile right now."

She's not wrong.

Perhaps I've underestimated her.

I grab her by the forearms, squeezing hard. I sear my gaze into her. "Then show me your volatility, Raven. Show me now. Take off those clothes and get on the fucking bed."

15

RAVEN

I obey him without hesitation. I pull my T-shirt over my head, exposing my bra and breasts. He sucks in a breath, and I can't help a small smile.

My nipples are hard and searching. I ache for his lips around them.

I kick off my flip-flops, and then I unsnap and unbuckle my jeans, sliding them over my hips and down my legs. I step out of them. Only my panties—red cotton—lie between me and total nudity.

I fling my thumbs underneath the waistband and slide them over my hips.

And I watch Vinnie as he looks at me.

Through his eyes I see my body for what it is. It's not too thin, and it's not hairless.

To him, it's a bounty. Something he yearns for, just as much as I yearn for him.

"Raven," he says, his voice dark.

I lift my eyebrows.

"I believe I told you to get on the fucking bed."

I turn, walk toward the king-size bed that's covered in what looks like burgundy silk. I sit down, and it's soft and cool against my body.

"Spread your fucking legs."

Again, I obey, baring my pussy to his view.

He kneels next to the bed, still fully clothed in his suit and tie. He moves his head between my legs, his stubble tickling my sensitive thighs.

He closes his eyes, inhales. "Damn, you smell good." Then he slides his fingers over my pussy. "Wet, too. You're wet for me, Raven."

Am I supposed to respond? Of course I'm wet for him. I ache for him.

"I'm so hard for you right now," he says. "I've never gotten as hard for a woman as I get for you. I could fuck you right now, Raven. I could fuck you and fuck you and fuck you and never get tired of the sweet suction of your cunt." He takes a deep breath in through his nose and exhales through his mouth, his eyes fiery. "But first I want to lick you. I want to eat you raw. I want to make you come. Then I want to make you come again. I want to flip you over, slide my tongue against your asshole, and then devour your pussy and make you come a third time."

I gulp audibly. "I'm not stopping you."

"There's no stopping me now, Raven." He lowers his head. "No fucking stopping me."

He slides his tongue over me, and my breath hitches. I close my eyes and grasp two fistfuls of the silk comforter.

I feel every touch of his tongue, of his lips, of his teeth on my most private parts. He's not gentle. He bites at me, nips at me, slides up to my clit and sucks hard.

I don't want gentle. I want what he needs. And he needs this.

I try not to think of the fact that he's going to let me go after this. Perhaps he'll realize he can't live without me.

But I know in my heart that won't happen. He thinks he needs to let me go to keep me safe, and that is at the forefront of his mind.

But safety isn't what I want.

I want Vinnie.

I *need* Vinnie.

"I want you to come for me," he says against my sensitive flesh. "Come for me, Raven." Then he slides his tongue over my clit, closes his lips around it, and sucks.

And I shatter.

Pieces of me float all over this bedroom as every cell in my body vibrates, culminates in my pussy, and then moves outward, like a rock thrown in the ocean, circling outward, outward, outward...

His fingers are inside of me, touching my G-spot, circling as my walls pulse around them.

The climax becomes me. I become it.

We are one and the same.

From high above I hear Vinnie's voice.

"God, Raven," he breathes. "You're so fucking hot. God, I love you."

I plummet back into my body, and he meets my gaze from between my legs. "Ready to go again?"

"Like I said," I reply, my voice raspy with need, my breath

coming in rapid pants, "I can take everything you want to dish out."

His smile is almost wicked as he moves back to my body, his lips hot against my skin. His fingers trail a lingering path, teasing my sensitive flesh until I'm practically writhing beneath him.

"I know you can, Raven," he murmurs. "But can you take it again? And again?" He moves his fingers expertly inside me once more, toying with that spot that makes me see stars.

I gasp at the sudden pleasure, my nails digging into his shoulders as I murmur a breathless "Yes."

He moves upward and his lips meet mine in a hot, desperate kiss that tastes of sweat and desire and all things Vinnie. He nips at my lower lip and slides his tongue against mine in a rhythm that mirrors his fingers in my pussy.

He pulls away just slightly, enough to whisper heatedly in my ear. "Good, because I won't stop until you're begging for it."

His voice is like velvet, sensual and demanding. Every word he breathes against my skin sends another wave of heat shooting through me. He's relentless, exploring every inch of my body, his mouth leaving a trail of scorching kisses in its wake.

"You're mine," he growls against my skin, a possessive command that only serves to further fuel the fire raging within me. "Only mine, Raven."

I nod frantically, too lost in the moment to form words. His dark eyes lock onto mine, a predatory gleam in their depths that makes my heart pound even harder.

He slides back down and tongues my pussy again.

And again.

Until I'm soaring once more, over the Texas plains, running, running, running...

I thread my fingers through his silky hair—so soft, like wheatgrass, but the color of the darkest night.

"Come, come, come..." he commands against my thighs.

When the orgasm subsides, he plunges his fingers into me again, scissoring them so that they hit every spot in perfect harmony.

And I come.

I come.

I come.

Until my body is quivering beneath him, my mind in the stars.

In front of me, as my climax surges through me, I see him. His clothes. Gone. On the floor.

Naked. Naked Vinnie. Big hard cock. Beautiful cock.

He walks toward me, moves his hands to my hips, gripping them tightly as he thrusts into me, his rhythm unyielding and raw. The room fills with the sounds of our heavy breathing, our bodies slapping against each other while he plunges in and out of me, setting every nerve on fire. The last climax morphs into another—this one more profound with the joining of our bodies.

"No one else," I manage to choke out, my fingers digging into his back. "Only you, Vinnie."

A feral grin blooms across his face at my declaration. His movements grow more forceful, relentless, pushing me toward another precipice I'm more than willing to tumble over.

"Say it again," he demands breathlessly.

"Only you," I gasp out as he guides me ever closer to another explosion I can sense is going to be earth-shattering. "Vinnie...on—"

The climax hits me hard, washing over me like a tidal wave that sucks the air from my lungs and leaves me shaking in its wake.

Vinnie's low growl of satisfaction echoes in my ears as he follows, his own orgasm rippling through him with a ferocity that shakes the bed beneath us. He collapses onto me, his sweat-slicked body heavy and comforting.

"Raven..." he whispers, his voice raspy from exertion. "God, I could do this forever."

"What," I choke out, still trying to recollect the fragmented bits of my sanity, "makes you think I'd stop you?"

His laughter is warm against my skin. It's a sound I hear so rarely that it sends a pang through my chest. We lie there for what feels like an eternity, our breaths mingling, the only sounds our racing heartbeats.

He pulls back slightly, just enough to look into my eyes. "You're right," he says softly, barely more than a whisper. "There's no stopping now."

He lays his head against my chest once more, and I feel the rhythm of his breath syncing with my own. He wraps his arms around me tightly, as if he's trying to pull me into him. Our bodies are so entwined that it's hard to tell where I end and he begins.

He traces lazy circles across my stomach and down my hip, a mindless pattern that soothes my still-tingling skin. I let my hands wander through his dark hair, untangling the mess our passionate encounter has made of it.

"Vinnie," I whisper. "Thank you."

He lifts his head to look at me, a puzzled expression on his face that makes me smile despite the tears prickling in the corners of my eyes. "For what?"

I swallow hard and reach up to caress his face. His stubble pricks my fingers, adding another layer of Vinnie to my senses. "For nothing," I reply. "And for everything."

He pulls me into a tender kiss that feels like a balm to my soul. He understands.

"You should get some rest," he murmurs, his warm breath tickling my bald head. "I need to get you home."

I shake my head against his chest. I'm not ready for this moment to end. I know what awaits me—the separation, the goodbye. I want to hold onto him just a little longer.

"Raven," he whispers after a few moments of silence. "You need to rest," he says again. "You're still recovering from your cancer, and after what happened at your parents' home..."

His voice trails off, and I can feel the tension stiffen his body.

"I'll rest later." I press a soft kiss against his chest. "Right now, I just want to be here with you."

"But—"

"Vinnie," I cut him off, leaning up to look him in the eyes. "This is what I need right now."

He studies me for a moment before surrendering with a sigh.

I tangle my fingers through his hair once more, letting my eyelids grow heavy as I listen to the rhythmic thump of his heart. He strokes up and down my arm in slow, soothing motions, lulling me into a calm state.

"I love you, Raven."

Tears well up in my eyes at his words, but I blink them

back, not wanting to start crying now. After all we've been through, after everything that's happened, those three words mean more to me than anything in this world.

"I love you too, Vinnie," I whisper back, my voice choked with emotion.

16

VINNIE

There's nothing I'd like more than to give Raven the rest she deserves, but I need to make sure her parents know she's safe. After what happened at their home...

They must be freaking out.

Her eyes are closed, and she looks so peaceful, so serene. I feather my hands over the contours of her beautiful face. So creamy and smooth.

"Raven, baby?"

She opens her eyes. "Yeah? Did I fall asleep?"

I kiss her cheek. "You need to go home now."

Her lip quivers. "I want to stay with you, Vinnie. You make me feel so safe."

God, those words... If only they were true. There's nothing I want more in the world than to keep this woman safe. This amazing woman whose life I care for more than my own.

But the fact of the matter is that she's not safe with me. She's in danger with me.

"Your parents are going to be worried about you. Especially in light of everything else that's happened. But I don't want you driving home alone."

She frowns. "I made it here, didn't I?"

"You did, but it will be dark soon. So what I need you to do right now, Raven, is to call your mother. She's probably been trying to reach you. Let her know that you're okay, and then I will drive you home. My driver, Fred, will follow us in my car. Then he'll drive me back."

She squints at the time on the alarm clock on the nightstand. "But it will be so late when you get back here."

"That doesn't matter, Raven. What matters is that you're safe. I don't want you driving all that way alone. You shouldn't have done it today."

"But Vinnie, I had to see you."

I inhale slowly, run my fingers through my hair. "God, Raven. This is so hard for me. Why are you doing this?"

She drops her jaw, and I immediately regret my words.

I hold up a hand. "No, I'm not blaming you. It's not your fault that you're so wonderful and beautiful and I fell head over heels in love with you." I sigh, looking down. "If only we hadn't met."

She gasps. "You don't really mean that, do you?"

I blink for a moment before responding. "Of course not."

Because in reality I don't, but how can I explain it to her that part of me wishes we hadn't met? Because then she would be safe. Safe to recover and live the long life she deserves. We would be blissfully unaware of the life-changing passion we experience with each other, and we wouldn't be drawn together despite every lethal threat that she faces.

If I could keep her safe, I would. But as long as my grandfather is still in control of the family—and he knows my feelings for Raven—she's *not* safe. You'd think, after what was done to his true love, Serena, he would hesitate to put his own flesh and blood through the same thing.

But that's not how Mario Bianchi lives his life. He lives his life through fear and manipulation. It doesn't matter if you're his own flesh and blood. That's how he gets what he wants.

I suppose the one thing he couldn't have was Serena.

So instead of learning from that mess and becoming a good man, he let it eat away everything good inside him. All that love he had for Serena has now been turned to snakelike evil.

Raven wipes a tear from her cheek. "Please don't ever say that again. Because I swear to God. I love my life. I do. But I'd rather live one moment of wonderful than a lifetime of nothing special. And you, Vinnie, are wonderful."

She's killing me.

I place my hands over hers. "Raven, my feelings for you will never change. Tell me you believe that."

"I do. Mine for you will never change either."

I nod. That's not what I'm after.

I grab her hands, remove them from my face. "I'm glad to know that, but it's imperative that you remember that. That whatever happens, you remember that I love you. I will never stop loving you. Whether we're together or not."

She opens her mouth but closes it abruptly.

Was she going to argue with me? Has she now decided to accept what I'm saying?

Finally she speaks. "You were wrong to leave me the other

night, Vinnie. You were wrong to leave me alone in my bed at my place."

I nod slowly. "I know that. And Raven, I don't want you living alone. Not until your safety can be guaranteed."

"Well, it's a good thing I was at my own home that night," she says. "What if *I* was the target? What if the hit on Brick was meant for me?"

For the first time, I allow myself to think of that possibility.

More like a probability.

Especially with the note that was left.

I haven't told Raven that *Cobra* refers to my grandfather. Or to me.

Only three people know I was once called Cobra. One is in prison. One is dead, buried under the Bellamys' old barn.

And the third one?

My esteemed grandfather.

I haven't had the chance to confront him about Brick Latham's death. Perhaps there's something I don't know. Perhaps Brick was on some kind of hit list.

But I doubt it.

Even if Raven wasn't the intended target, Brick's death is a message to me.

A message that my grandfather is still in control, and that I'd better play the game by his rules.

17

RAVEN

I do as Vinnie asks.

I get up, get dressed, and find my phone. As he suspected, there are several calls from my mother. Several texts as well. She wants to know where I am, if I'm safe.

I consider texting her back, but knowing my mother that won't be enough. She'll get it in her head that someone has my phone and is texting in my stead.

So I call her.

"Oh my God, Raven, thank goodness. Where are you?"

"I had to go somewhere, Mom. But don't worry. I'm going to be home in a couple of hours."

"Raven, please. What are you up to? After everything that's gone on..."

Maybe I should be straight with her. Maybe I should tell her that I'm in love with Savannah's brother. Maybe. I already told Falcon and Leif. I told Savannah.

But I can't.

"Just trust me, Mom. Please."

"Raven, you know very well it's not a question of trust. Of course I trust you. You're a mature adult." Her voice cracks. "But after almost losing you... I suppose I'm destined to worry about you until my dying day. After everything Falcon went through, and then you... And now this. Someone getting into our home. Our sacred space. Murdering that poor attorney."

"I know. Have the police contacted you again?"

"No, not yet. If they need any of us to make a formal statement at the station, I'm sure they will let us know."

"I suppose it's a good sign that we haven't been called yet," I say.

"Yes, definitely a good thing. Your father's beside himself. Even this new security system that your brother and Leif got installed hasn't helped."

"I understand. His space has been violated. Yours was too. And mine. It's disorienting. But that's nothing compared to what happened to Mr. Latham."

"I know, honey. I know."

"I'll be home soon, Mom. So don't worry, okay?"

"I'll try not to. And I won't ask you where you went."

"Thank you for that. I appreciate it. I appreciate your trust."

"Just stay safe, honey."

"I will, Mom. Goodbye. I love you."

"I love you too, sweetheart."

I end the call.

Vinnie has dressed, and he's waiting for me at the front door of the guesthouse.

"You ready?" he asks.

I'm not sure how to answer that question. Am I ready to

go home? Yes. I need to go home. For my mother's sake. For my father's. They need to know I'm safe.

But am I ready to leave?

That's another question altogether.

Because when I leave, I don't know when—or if—I'll see Vinnie again.

"Sure," I finally say. "Let's go."

He looks at me then, meets my gaze, and his own dark eyes are so beautiful and troubled. I want to lean into him, lean against his hard body, show him that everything will be okay.

But I don't know that it will be.

And neither does he.

If only we could go away. Far from here. Start over.

I open my mouth to say as much, but then I close it.

"What do you want to say, Raven?" he asks.

"Would anything I say make a difference?"

"You mean change our lives right now? Make it so we can be together?"

I nod.

He sighs. "I wish I could say it would, Raven. You have no idea how much I wish that."

"So that's your answer?"

"You want me to be specific about it? No, Raven. Nothing you can say will make any difference."

"Then I suppose there's nothing to say."

And there isn't. We don't speak for the rest of the drive.

I WAKE up the next morning in one of the guest bedrooms in my mother and father's house. I can't stomach the thought of being in my own room—where a man was found bleeding out on my bed.

It's still a crime scene anyway. It will be until the police close the investigation.

So far, the police aren't questioning my parents and me any further.

I don't know whether that's because they believe our alibis or because my father is who he is.

He's a good man. He doesn't own the police station or anything.

But he does know them all. The two policemen who were here the other day—Detective Harrison and Officer Martinez—are young. Probably about my own age, though the detective may be a few years older.

My father has contacts everywhere, so it's reasonable for me to believe he has contacts with the police who will see that no charges are levied against anyone in my family.

But then I wonder...

If my father had that kind of power, why did Falcon go to prison?

We were told at the time that two factors were in play. Number one, the Bellamy name. It was a good chance to make an example of Falcon, to show that no one is above the law, no matter what his name is.

But more so, it was because a young rookie cop was dead. Not only that, but Jaden Perez left behind a pregnant wife.

Public sympathy had never been higher.

It was around ten o'clock when Vinnie drove my car into my parents' drive.

No kiss good night, though he did walk me to the door.

Then he parked my car in the driveway, got into his own car with Fred at the wheel, and drove away.

My mother was waiting up for me in the kitchen, of course. Dad was in the study.

I saw my mother, kissed her cheek, told her I was fine, and went to bed in the guest room.

This morning I'm up early, and I head into the kitchen where my mother stands at the stove, staring into space.

"You okay, Mom?" I ask.

She nods.

But she's lying. How can she be okay? My mother has been to hell and back. First with Falcon, and then with me and my illness. And now with this horrific crime that took place in our own home. Maybe our lunch yesterday helped a little...but only a little.

Finally, she gathers her composure. "Breakfast, Ray?"

"Sure, Mom. Two eggs, scrambled. Toast."

My mother robotically prepares my breakfast. I want to tell her I can fix my own breakfast, or that I'm not hungry—which I'm not, but I know I'll eat anyway. But she needs her routine. She thrives on it.

She prepares my breakfast and places it in front of me on the table, along with her signature tall glass of orange juice.

I drink it all without complaint.

I'll pay for it later with the heartburn, but it makes Mom happy.

"I think I'll try to contact another attorney about my nonprofit," I say once I'm done with my breakfast.

Mom jerks around, looking me straight in the eye. "You're still going to do that?"

"Yeah, I think so. I considered not doing it, in light of what happened to Mr. Latham. I thought maybe I would go back to school. But no. I want to do my nonprofit. I've already thought of a name for it."

"Oh?" Mom's tone is noncommittal.

"Yeah. Raven's Wings. Isn't that a great name?"

"You're naming it after yourself?"

I purse my lips. "Is that not good?"

She blinks for a moment and then shakes her head. "I'm sorry, honey. Raven's Wings is a great name. I don't know what's gotten into me."

She doesn't need to explain herself. I know exactly what's gotten into her, and so does she.

I place a hand on her upper arm. "Mom, everything's going to be okay."

She closes her eyes, takes a deep breath in, and then sighs. "Raven, I don't want you in this position. I don't want you in a position where you're telling *me* that everything's going to be okay. That's *my* job. I'm the mother here. I need to be taking care of you."

I chuckle lightly. "That would be true if I were five or ten. Or even eighteen. But I'm nearly thirty years old, Mom. Yes, I've been through hell. And yes, a crime was committed here in our home. A perfectly heinous and horrific crime. We're all rattled. Any sane person would be. So I think it's perfectly fine for *me* to do the soothing for a bit, Mom. We have to face what happened. Just like I had to face my illness, and we all had to face Falcon's incarceration. We'll face it head on, like we face everything else. And we can make it a heck of a lot easier if we support each other through it."

Mom smiles then. "You amaze me, Raven. Such internal strength you have."

I walk toward her and give her a hug.

I hate to tell her that she's wrong. She's wrong about my internal strength. I won't deny that I have it, but I don't have any more than anyone else. I've just had to rely on mine more than the average person. Because when push comes to shove, you play the hand you're dealt. To do anything else would be to give up.

And Bellamys don't give up.

18

VINNIE

I slam the door to my grandfather's office. "You fucking son of a bitch."

He clears his throat from behind his desk. "Good morning to you too, Vincent."

"*Your move, Cobra?* You had a man killed and placed in Raven Bellamy's bed. His throat slit. With a message. For *me*."

He folds his hands neatly in front of him. "I don't know what you're talking about."

I cross the office and pound my fists against the wood of his desk. "That's a crock, and we both know it. It's probably all over the news."

"If it happened at the Bellamys' home? No, it's not all over the news." He strokes his chin. "They kept their son's incarceration quiet eight years ago. It was only on local news, and that was only because a cop was killed. The killer's name was rarely mentioned."

"This time it's not a cop. It's an attorney. An attorney from here in Austin. So I'm sure you've heard the news."

He looks up at me, his face wholly noncommittal. "And what makes you think I'm involved?"

I roll my eyes. "You really think you're smart, don't you? You really think that you're so big and powerful that no one will ever challenge you. You left a note, Grandpa. You know damned well you left a note. That note was for me."

"Because it said 'Cobra?'"

"Yep. And we both know that the only person who ever called me *Cobra* was Diego Vega, who's dead. And the only other person who heard him say that was *you*."

"And your own father," Grandfather says.

"Yeah." I stare at him from across the desk. "And I bet it was really easy for him to get out of prison and arrange a hit on a lawyer at the Bellamys' house."

He lets out a choking laugh. "You can't blame me for trying."

"Were you going to try to get Raven? Except that she wasn't there?"

He crosses his arms. "Why would you ask me that?"

"Because the lawyer, Brick Latham, was going to the Bellamys' home to see Raven."

"And you think he was just in the wrong place at the wrong time," Grandfather says. A statement, not a question.

"I don't know." I slink down in the chair behind me. "I don't know how your warped mind works, which is a good thing from where I'm standing. Either the hit was for Raven, or there's some reason you hit this Brick Latham. Did he do something to piss off the family?"

"As far as I know, Mr. Latham was an upstanding attorney at a law firm whose biggest client is Austin Bellamy and the Bellamy Ranch."

"Yeah. And he just *happened* to be helping Raven Bellamy with a nonprofit organization she wants to start. And he just happened to have a date with her Friday night."

He smirks. "I'm thinking he's regretting that choice about now."

"He can't regret anything, Grandfather. The dead have no regrets."

He widens his eyes and claps his hands. "Vincent, that was profound. I like it. I can see it engraved on a plaque somewhere in this office. *The dead have no regrets.*"

Anger crawls up the back of my neck. "You need to leave her alone. You need to leave the Bellamy family alone. Savannah's a member of that family now, Grandfather. And if you have any speck of love left for your only granddaughter, leave them the fuck alone."

He shakes his head. "This isn't about them, Vincent. It never was."

"No. I understand that." I pound a fist against my chest. "It's about *me*. It's *my* move. What if my move is to take you out, Grandfather?"

"You're not armed."

"No one gets into this office armed. Do you think I need anything other than my own two hands to squeeze the life out of you, old man?" I raise a fist.

He doesn't so much as flinch. "I can have three goons in here in the next second if you even attempt to try."

I don't doubt his words. Still, the other day, I grabbed him by his collar and pulled him toward me, threatening him, and he didn't call his goons.

Which means he doesn't consider me a threat.

He should reconsider that stance.

"So go ahead and try, Vincent," he goads me.

"Stay the hell away from the Bellamys and I won't have to."

He cocks his head. "You expect me to stay away from them, yet you don't. The lovely Ms. Bellamy showed up at your mother's house last night."

"She did." I don't bother to lie. He's obviously having me watched. "But she came of her own accord."

"You didn't make her leave."

"No, I didn't." I stand up again. "I'm not a fucking asshole. She had dinner with Mom and me. And Mom loved her, by the way."

He scoffs. "Your mother is useless."

"My mother is your only child, old man."

He doesn't reply.

Why should he? We both know she is.

We both know he was disgusted that his wife could only give him one child, and a girl at that.

"My mother is still my mother," I say. "And you will treat her with respect."

"Whether I deem her worthy of my respect depends on you, Vincent."

"Why would your respect for my mother have anything to do with me?" I ask. "She's your child, damn it. She gave you three grandchildren. That alone should make her worthy of your respect."

He shrugs. "We'll see, Vincent. We'll see."

"Fine. Hate my mother. Hate the whole fucking world for all I care. Just stay away from the Bellamys."

He raises an eyebrow. "If you stay away from them, so will I."

He wants me to say it. He wants me to stay away from Raven. I'll try like hell, but I can't control what she does. That woman does whatever the hell she wants. I wish I could be annoyed by her stubbornness, but I actually find it a pretty attractive trait.

I narrow my gaze at my grandfather. "So that's the deal? You leave them alone if *I* do?"

"That's the deal."

"I don't buy it, pops. Savannah is a Bellamy now. And I'm not staying away from my sister."

He frowns. "Then don't expect the Bellamys to get a free pass. Savannah made her choice. Now you need to make yours, Vincent."

Chills skitter over my flesh.

I'm used to my grandfather making demands of me. I'm used to his serpentine horror. I'm used to him ordering me around, and I'm used to him not trusting me.

Has he truly turned his back on Savannah?

And what about his daughter? And her husband, my father?

"I want my sister in my life," I say.

"Do you? Does your mother?"

I hesitate to speak on that. While I know my mother loves Savannah, she blames her for me being in the position that I'm in.

My grandfather continues, "Caroline made her choice. She chose to love your father. Your father chose to love her. But love is an illusion, Vincent. All it does is make you weak."

I decide to play his own game here.

"Did your love for Serena make you weak?"

His forehead twitches. "Weaker than anything else. And I

paid for it. But Serena paid for it more than you can even imagine."

"Oh, I can imagine."

"Can you?" He throws his hands onto his desk and leans forward. "Because what I did to you after you turned eighteen was *nothing* compared to what they did to Serena. Hell, what my own father and his goons did to me was nothing in comparison either."

"Well, she's dead now," I say, "and like I said. The dead have no regrets."

His face darkens. "I never said she was dead."

I stop my jaw from dropping. "You're telling me Serena is still alive?"

"I'm telling you that you will never know one way or the other."

Though my grandfather refuses to look away, I see a hair of regret in his eyes. He played his hand too soon. If Serena is alive—my grandfather still has a weakness.

A weakness I can exploit.

But I'm not the same man he is.

I will never exploit an elderly woman—one who's probably been through torturous hell—just to bring down my grandfather.

But that doesn't mean I can't make him *think* I will.

So I meet his gaze—stare him down—until he finally looks away.

He hasn't claimed responsibility for the attorney's death at the Bellamy house, but I know damned well he's guilty.

Now is the chance to bring up something else I need help with.

I take a seat, never removing my gaze from the bastard who sired my mother.

"So grandfather," I say, "about Belinda McAllister..."

19

RAVEN

I knock lightly on my father's door to his study.

"Who is it?"

"It's me, Daddy. Raven."

"Come in, sweetie."

I walk in to see my father on his cell phone. "I have to go, Connor. I'll be back in touch."

"Was that one of our attorneys?" I ask.

"Yeah. Looks like we don't have anything to worry about with that dead lawyer. The police believe our alibis, and there are other more likely suspects in his murder. I just had a very interesting conversation with one of my attorneys who works at his firm, and it turns out the firm was looking for a way to get rid of him anyway."

I drop my jaw. "Daddy?"

He frowns. "I didn't mean for that to be as callous as it sounded, sweetheart. But frankly, we don't need this mess right now. I've already got the EPA breathing down my neck about the excavation of that land near the border. Those federal agencies are a big pain in the ass."

I keep my face noncommittal. I still don't know what Falcon and the guys plan to do. At some point they'll have to get in there and make sure the body of Diego Vega and all those drugs are gone. Then what will they do with the remains? I have no idea. Maybe it's better that I don't.

I swallow. "I understand, Daddy. But in light of what happened, I need to ask you for another referral."

"For an attorney, I understand. For your nonprofit."

I nod. "Right."

"I'll find you someone good." Then he sighs, rakes his fingers through his graying blond hair. "Are you sure you're up for this right now, honey? With everything going on... The death of that lawyer... In your bed..."

"You just said we don't need to worry about that."

"We don't need to worry about the police investigating," he says. "They've accepted our stories as true."

"Why shouldn't they? Our stories *are* true."

"They are, honey, but there are holes in them." He scratches at his chin. "Your mother and I didn't notice the body until the next morning, and you were alone at your place for part of the night. I know none of us had anything to do with that lawyer stuff, but..."

"But what, Daddy?"

He shakes his head. "Never mind, Raven. What's most important is your wellbeing. Are you feeling okay, honey?"

"I'm feeling fine."

Physically, that is. Mentally I'm a mess. At least I didn't have to look at the dead body. It will be a long time before I can sleep in that room again. If I ever do. All the more reason for me to move back into my own home. Especially since

Falcon has arranged for some big bodyguard to live there with me.

"All right. I suppose it will help for you to have something to focus on. I'll get you another attorney right away, sweetheart. In the meantime, you know you can count on your mother and me for anything you need. Money, support, whatever."

I slowly rise. "I'm sure I'll need all of those things. Thanks, Daddy."

He nods and picks up his phone.

That's my cue to leave.

CJ and I didn't get to have our visit on Sunday. The cops were still milling around.

Maybe I could go see her again.

I grab my phone out of my pocket and give her a call.

"Hey, Raven," she says into the phone. Her voice is a little bit off.

"Hey, CJ. Sorry I had to cancel on you Sunday."

"It's okay." She pauses. "Things are...a mess here."

"Yeah? What's going on?"

"Well, you'll notice I didn't text you back when I got your text about Sunday."

I honestly hadn't noticed. But I was obviously otherwise occupied. "Yeah, I know."

"Mr. P—my boss..."

"Yeah?"

"He's... He's...uh...dead."

The phone falls from my hand and lands on the carpeted hallway with a soft thud. I pick it back up quickly. "Oh my God, CJ. What's going on?"

I haven't told CJ about the dead lawyer in my bed. They couldn't possibly be related, could they?

"When did it happen?"

"The forensic team thinks it happened sometime Friday night."

My blood runs cold. Friday night is when Brick Latham was killed. Murdered, and then placed in my bed.

My mind races. This is all way too much of a coincidence...

"Oh my God."

"Yeah. He was in Houston on business. The maids found him dead in his hotel room Saturday morning. But like I said, the forensics team thinks the time of death was sometime Friday evening."

"Does this mean you're out of a job, CJ?"

"Not necessarily. I don't know yet. Mrs. Puzo is busy taking care of the details, of course, and the girls... Well, they know their father's dead. But they weren't very close to him, hardly ever saw him. I've been spending a lot of time with them, trying to get them to understand what's going on, but without upsetting them."

"Isn't that what their mother should be doing?"

CJ scoffs through the phone. "In a perfect world, yes. But she's such a socialite. Not even the death of her husband can disrupt her schedule. She's not really their mother. In name only, if you know what I mean. She barely knows them."

I don't know what CJ means. My parents were hands-on. They taught me everything I know about ranch work, homemaking, and how to be a good person.

"So anyway, what's going on with you? Why did you have to cancel?"

"You're not even going to believe this," I say. "But do you remember that date I had with that lawyer?"

"Yeah."

"I ended up canceling it at the last minute, because I was with—"

"You were with Vincent Gallo."

I nearly drop the phone again. "I..."

Her voice gets playful again. The CJ I remember. "Don't try to deny it, Ray. I saw the sizzling chemistry between you when he showed up at the Puzos' home. I knew you had sex. And who could blame you? The man's a stud."

God. Vinnie. The Puzos' home. He was there, asking to see CJ's boss. He had no idea I would be there.

Is he behind Mr. Puzo's death?

Oh God...

"Ray? You there?"

I quickly gather my wits. "Yes, I'm here. And yes, there was something between Vinnie and me, but no longer. The point is that I broke the date with the lawyer, but he didn't get my text in time and he ended up at our house."

"Oh, talk about awkward."

"It was way more than awkward, Ceej. He..." I gulp back the nausea that threatens to erupt out of my throat. "Someone killed him, CJ. Someone killed him."

She gasps through the phone. "Oh my God."

I leave out the part about him being found with his throat slit in my bed. That's too horrible to even think about, let alone say.

Plus, my father will keep as much of this quiet as he can. But he can't keep the death quiet. There will be an obituary.

He was a young man, had his whole life ahead of him. People will mourn him.

"I wasn't home," I say. "Neither were my mom and dad. They had gone out for the evening."

"My God, I'm so sorry."

"Thanks. I'm sorry about Mr. Puzo, too."

She sighs. "I hardly know him. *Knew* him. I think I met him twice. He kind of had a greasy look about him, if you know what I mean."

"Oh?"

"Yeah. Mrs. Puzo is a lot younger than he was. She's beautiful. The match didn't make a lot of sense in my book. But of course the house they live in... I might be able to sleep with some greasy guy if it meant I could live in this house."

"Well, she won't have to sleep with him anymore."

"Nope. She seems distraught, for real. But it could all be an act. I don't know. It's not like I ever saw them spending any time together, and I live here twenty-four-seven. He was almost never home, and like I said, they kept their bedroom locked."

"Well, I was going to ask if you want to get together, but I'm pretty sure you're busy."

"Yeah, I am. Anna and Paulina are staying home from school this week, so I'm on duty full time. Once all the dust settles, I'm not sure if I'll still have a job."

"I'm sure Mr. Puzo left Mrs. Puzo very well taken care of. And she'll still have all of her causes and societies. The kids will still need a caretaker. My guess is you'll still have a job."

"True. The question is whether I want it. I love the girls, but all of a sudden this house feels strange to me. Like ghosts are watching me or something."

I rub my arms against the chill that erupts. "Yeah, I know what you mean. When someone dies, it feels that way."

"Maybe this weekend though," she says. "I still have Sundays off."

"Okay. We'll set it tentatively. But I understand if you need to cancel."

"Ditto," she says. "Take care, Ray."

"You too." The call ends with a soft click.

No sooner does CJ hang up when my phone rings again.

It's Falcon.

20

VINNIE

"What about Belinda McAllister?" Grandfather asks.

"I'd like to talk about...taking a more active role in her life."

Grandfather raises one eyebrow. "Vincent, I didn't know you had those inclinations."

I feel sick. I could upchuck right now, right on my grandfather's smug face.

I swallow it down. I won't give this bastard the pleasure of a violent reaction. "I don't have any such *inclinations*, Grandfather, and you're disgusting to even think that. But if the woman is to be my wife, perhaps she should come live with Mom and me. In her own room, with her nanny."

God, I sound like a first-class creep.

Grandfather's eyebrows are still raised. "Declan will never go for that."

I sink into my chair. "Which is why you need to convince him."

"Convince him?" He scowls. "He'll think you're a fucking

child molester, Vinnie. We're lucky we have such a good alliance with the McAllisters at all, considering that your father killed one of them."

I'm not sure what to say to my grandfather. If I tell him that Declan is hurting Belinda, he won't care. It's par for the course in his world.

"I think it would be good for my mother," I say. "She's very lonely."

"And you don't think Declan would be lonely without his daughter?"

I jump to my feet. "I don't fucking care if Declan will be lonely. Right now he's hurting her."

Grandfather's expression doesn't change.

Just as I thought.

"And you know this how?"

I can't tell him. I can't tell him that Belinda gave me a note and that I talked to the nanny. If I do that, he'll go straight to Declan, and both Belinda and the nanny will pay the price.

"Never mind." I cross my arms. "I'm sure she's fine where she is."

"Yes, I'm sure she is as well." He strokes his chin. "Do me a favor, Vincent."

"What now?"

"Forget about what you think you might know about the child." He leers over the desk. "And in return, I am going to forget *you* ever brought this up. Do we understand each other?"

I look into my grandfather's cold, watery eyes. Yes, we understand each other perfectly. He knows what's going on with Belinda, and he doesn't care.

And he knows someone breached a confidence, which is how *I* know.

So he'll keep quiet... As long as *I* let it lie.

"Yes, we understand each other." I keep my expression noncommittal.

But inside I'm raging. How can he let a young girl suffer? And am I supposed to do that as well? She asked for my help.

No, she *begged* for it.

And Natalie is risking her job—and probably her life—by trying to protect her little charge.

That little girl should not be in this situation.

She should be working toward a scholarship to Juilliard. For a career as a concert pianist. All that talent will go to waste. She's being raised to be a quiet child-rearing Mafia wife.

This life is not fair.

It's not fair to anyone.

Even to my grandfather. I don't feel sorry for the old bastard, but watching the love of his life suffer could not have been easy. No wonder he had to let his heart turn to stone.

I'll have to find another way to help Belinda. Without my grandfather's—or Declan's—knowledge.

A plan begins to percolate in my mind.

I don't know if I'll be able to pull it off, but...

"If there's nothing else, Grandfather..."

"There is, actually," he says. "I need you to go to Colombia."

I cock my head slowly. "What for?"

His lip twitches. "That will be made clear to you soon enough."

My instinct is to push him on this. To tell him he's insane

if he thinks I'm going to fly off to Colombia without even knowing what my assignment will be when I get there.

But then I think of that poor little girl. And how the man in front of me might be my only shot at giving her the help she needs.

I nod slowly. "Not a problem. I'll make arrangements."

He slides a portfolio across the desk to me. "Arrangements are already made. You leave this evening."

I pull out the portfolio. Inside is an itinerary and an e-ticket receipt. Everything looks to be in order, except—

"I'm going to be gone for a *month?*" I say.

"That's what it says, Vincent."

I shove the portfolio back at him. "No way. I'm not going to be gone that long. Especially if you're not even telling me what I'm going to be doing there."

Grandfather folds his hands in front of him. "I'm afraid you don't have a choice in the matter, Vincent. With Puzo's demise, there are some loose ends to take care of, and you being out of the country will serve you well while the investigation into his death is going on. You're going to go to Columbia as a representative of this family. You're going to take care of the business Giacomo Puzo no longer can."

I frown. "Puzo didn't work for our family."

A small grin cracks across his face. "No, but I want the piece of the pie he was trying to take. Plus..."

I groan. "What?"

"There's some...cargo I need you to take care of."

"You can ship your own damned drugs, Grandpa. And your own damned coffee beans for that matter. At least that's legal."

"This cargo isn't drugs. Or coffee." His expression remains unchanged.

My breath catches in my throat. "No. No way."

"It's your job, Vincent."

I shake my head. "How were you ever talked into this, Grandfather? After nearly a century of this family business. Sure, we're criminals, but we drew the line at people."

He narrows his eyes. "So you're saying it's moral to bring drugs over the border and get people hooked. Be responsible for overdoses, the deaths of thousands. But it's not moral to bring people across the border? People who are only looking for a better life?"

"And what better life do you plan to give them? Life in servitude. *Sexual* servitude, most likely."

"A life where they'll be well fed and taken care of," he says.

"You're the devil," I say.

"Don't even begin to lecture me on morality, Vincent," he says. "There are no degrees of morality. There's just simply morality and immorality."

No.

Just no.

There *are* degrees. I have to believe that or I can't live with myself and what I've done.

But is he right?

Why was it easier for me to think about the business when it was only drugs? Despite all the damage drugs do to innocent people?

Is it all that different to just take the innocent people? Bring them into a better country from where they are, except that… I can't stomach the thought…

But if I do this… If I get my hands dirty, I may get some contacts that I need.

And perhaps those contacts can get Belinda out of the McAllister house for me.

This whole thing is making me want to throw up.

I may never eat again.

One thing is for sure. I need to make sure Raven understands that she and I are through. For good this time.

She's been through enough.

I can't get her involved in this.

21

RAVEN

"Hi, Falcon," I say into the phone.

"Hey, Ray. Can you meet me over at your place?"

"Yeah, I suppose so." I look around—the house is still. "Nothing much else going on over here."

"Great. See you there around ten."

I end the call and find my mother still in the kitchen, sitting at the table and nursing a cup of tea. Her normally rosy face is pale.

"You okay, Mom?"

She looks up at me and forces a smile. "Yes, of course, Raven."

"I'm going to go over to my place for a little while. Falcon wants me to meet him there."

"Whatever for?"

"He didn't say," I say, "and I didn't ask."

She sighs. "Raven..."

"Dad says we're in the clear about Mr. Latham's murder," I say.

She nods. "That's good news at least."

"Yes, it is." I walk toward her and give her a kiss on her cheek. Her cheek is cold. Her eyes are...spent. Like she has no tears left to cry.

This whole thing has her rattled. Maybe I shouldn't leave. But Falcon... I can't say no to him. Not ever. I literally owe him my life.

"I won't be gone long," I say. "And if I have to stay longer, I will give you a call."

"Thank you, Raven. I appreciate that." She takes a sip of her tea.

I inhale the steam coming from the tea. The earthy and floral aroma of chamomile. She's trying to relax.

I hope she can.

I sure as heck can't.

I go outside, get in my car, and drive the few minutes to my place.

Falcon's car is already there when I arrive, along with a car I don't recognize. A black Suburban.

I walk up to my door, enter the code, and go into my house.

Falcon sits in my kitchen along with a very large man. He's tall, at least six foot six, with dark skin and the build of about three linebackers.

"Raven, this is Jared. Jared Tucker. Your new bodyguard."

Jared stands—and he's even bigger than I thought he was. "Ms. Bellamy, it's a pleasure." He walks toward me and holds out his hand.

I take his hand, letting it dwarf my own. "Mr. Tucker."

"Call me Jared, ma'am."

"Sure." I let go of his hand. "And you may call me Raven. I don't like Ms. Bellamy, or God forbid"—I shudder—"*ma'am*."

He cracks a small smile. "Whatever you say, Raven."

"We were lucky to find Jared," Falcon says. "Leif knows him from the Navy."

"Oh, did you serve with Leif?"

Jared shakes his head. "Not in the way you mean. I was a SEAL, but Phoenix and I were with different companies. Everybody knew the Phoenix, though. He could get out of any trouble."

"So I've heard."

"He's a good man."

"Leif vouches for Jared also," Falcon adds. "And his word is as good as gold."

"I'm sure you're a perfectly nice man," I say to Jared. "And thank you for what you're doing for me."

He nods. "Thank you for the job. I will do my best to keep any harm from coming to you."

"I know."

I don't ask how much he's being paid. I'm sure it's a ton. I'll talk to Falcon about it later and make sure it comes out of my trust fund.

"I've arranged for Jared to stay in the room right next to yours," Falcon says.

"Sure, that's fine."

"You have nothing to fear from having me here," Jared says.

"I don't fear you."

"You don't want to fear me," he says, "but it's clear on your face when you look at me. I know what I look like, how large I am. I'm used to the stares."

I drop my gaze to the floor. "I apologize."

"Don't. There's no need for that. Your brother and Leif have apprised me of the situation. Any person would have their guard up after what you and your family have been through. I would be shocked if you didn't." He gestures out the kitchen window toward my driveway. "I'll be your driver as well. You saw my SUV outside. Where you go, I go."

I turn to my brother. "Falcon..."

"Nonnegotiable," my brother says. "Until we get this shit settled."

I swallow. "Does he know everything?"

"I only know what I need to know, Raven," Jared says. "And all I need to know is that your safety is paramount and that's why I'm here."

I nod. "So...what if I want to go somewhere?"

"I'll drive you."

"What if I want to go visit Falcon and Savannah? Or my mom and dad?"

"I'll accompany you. If you want privacy, I'll stay in the car. Or I can stay elsewhere in the house while you're visiting. I assure you that I will be as discreet as possible while still ensuring your complete security."

"All right."

Falcon gives me a half hug around my shoulders. "This is all for your own safety."

I sigh. "Yes, I understand. Thank you for finding him, Falcon." I turn to Jared. "And thank you, Jared, for...whatever you're going to do, I guess."

He smiles. "What I'll be doing is protecting you, Raven." He taps the top of his thigh. "I'm armed at all times, and believe me. No one will get past me. You will be safe in my charge."

"You can take that to the bank, Ray," Falcon says. "Like I said, anyone who Leif recommends has my complete trust."

I give Jared another once-over. I don't doubt his words.

"So...I told my mom I'd come back to her house."

"Good enough," Jared says. "I'm happy to drive you over there."

I scratch my arm. "I don't know... This all feels... Violating, almost."

"I'll stay out of your personal space as much as I can," Jared says. "I can assure you that I am trained in keeping my clients as comfortable as they are safe. You won't even notice I'm there."

"We just had those top-of-the-line security systems put in all of our homes," I say. "Do I really need someone guarding me twenty-four-seven?"

"Yes, you do," Falcon says. "In light of everything, you do, Raven."

I swallow. He's no doubt right. What with the whole Diego Vega situation, and then Brick Latham's murder. And now CJ's boss, Mr. Puzo, who Vinnie was coming to see...

God, Vinnie...

I need to talk to him about this.

He'll no doubt be happy I have a bodyguard. In fact, it may have been his idea. Savannah is his sister, and I'm sure he talks to her as much as he talks to me. Probably more.

I jerk when my phone buzzes in my pocket. I pull it out.

It's Vinnie.

My heart nearly skips a beat.

"Would you two excuse me, please?" I walk out of the

kitchen and take some privacy in my living area. I accept the call and bring the receiver up to my ear.

"Vinnie?"

"I'm going out of town tonight, Raven."

"Oh?"

"Yes, and I'll be gone a long time. Probably about a month. I just wanted you to know so you won't try to get in touch with me."

A *month?*

My God, so much can happen in a month. I know Vinnie doesn't want to interact with me until after he's taken care of everything with his family, but some small part of me was hoping he would follow his heart and come back to me. If only for a discreet tryst every now and then.

But a month? That's so long.

"You there?" he asks.

"Yes." I bite my lip, searching for the right thing to say. "I… I'll miss you."

He says nothing.

I understand. He thinks the phone call may be monitored.

"Is this a…work trip?" I ask.

His voice darkens. "It is."

"Can you tell me where you're going at least? I mean, I assume they have cell coverage there. We can still talk."

He pauses before responding. "I'll be very busy, Raven. And no, I can't tell you where I'm going."

The phone clicks off.

Sadness sweeps through me. It seems every time I interact with Vinnie, he breaks my heart a little bit more. He didn't even say goodbye. Much less that he loves me. A lump begins to form in my throat, and I feel my bottom lip quiver.

But I swallow it back. I'm lucky to be alive, and I don't have time to waste on sadness.

This is my life now. A big man with guns who follows me everywhere. A super security system at my home.

This is my life.

But it's better than death.

22

VINNIE

I sit at the airport, getting ready to board my chartered flight to Bogotá.

My stomach feels sick, and I'm racking my brain to think of ways to get out of this when my phone rings.

"Is this Vincent Gallo?"

"Yes, who's this?"

"This is Officer Jett Davis with the Austin Police Department. I'm afraid I have some bad news about your mother."

My heart drops into my gut.

My mother?

Did my Grandfather really take out his frustrations toward me on his own daughter?

Oh, God. Oh, God...

"Shit. What happened?"

"She's had a heart attack. She's been transferred to Austin General. How soon can you get there?"

I look at my watch. "I'm supposed to get on a flight in ten minutes. But don't worry. Thank God I haven't gotten on yet. I'll be there as soon as I can."

I leave my luggage and hurry out of the airport, flagging down the first cab I see. Fred and my car are long gone. I give the cab driver the address and tell him to hurry.

Not fucking fast enough.

The whole ride I'm wondering what happened. My grandfather was just making veiled threats about my mother. I'm sure he has access to drugs or something that could mimic the symptoms of a heart attack.

But is he truly heartless enough to murder his own daughter?

He had Giacomo Puzo killed. A father of two.

Is a mother of three so different?

God, she could be dead. And this taxi driver is going the damn speed limit.

Savannah will be devastated. Should I call her?

No, she's probably already been contacted. And she doesn't need to hear from me while I'm freaking out.

Out of my hands.

Everything in my goddamned life is out of my hands, it seems.

My grandfather holds all the cards.

And maybe he's played the one I never thought he'd have the gall to do.

I jump out as soon as the cab comes to a stop in front of the hospital and run into the emergency room.

"Caroline Gallo?" I gasp out to the receptionist. "Heart attack."

"Are you family?"

"I'm her son. Vincent Gallo Junior."

"Of course, Mr. Gallo." She flags an orderly. "Please find a doctor. We need an update on Caroline Gallo."

"Yes. Of course. Have a seat, Mr. Gallo," the orderly says.

"No. I'm not going to sit down. Take me to my mother."

She gently wraps her hand around my arm, a sympathetic look on her face. "We have to check and see what's going on first. You can't just go running back—"

I break free of her arm and rush through the double doors.

The ER is busy tonight, and several people try to stop me, but I keep going. "Mom? Mom?"

Then I gasp.

Because behind curtain number three is...

My mother.

They're using the fucking paddles on her.

"Oh my God, Mom!"

The doctor turns and glares at me. "Get him out of here!"

A large man in scrubs grabs my arms. "I'm sorry, sir. You can't be in here."

"That's my mother."

He guides me toward the doors back to the waiting room. "I assure you that we're doing everything we can for her."

"I want answers." I grab him by the shoulders and shake him. "What the hell happened? Is she going to be all right?"

"The doctor will come talk to you as soon as he can." The man wriggles out of my grasp. "But we can only do that if the area is clear. For now, we need you to wait out here." He pushes me through the double doors.

I shrug free. "Keep your hands off me."

He raises his eyebrows, taken aback.

Damned right. I know what kind of presence I look like. I know my effect on people when I'm angry, determined.

"Sir..."

"Don't 'sir' me. I want some information on my mother."

"I'll see what I can find out. We're doing everything we can. But please...have a seat." He leans down. "I understand that you are upset, but it is an issue of safety for non-staff to be in the treatment area. If you come back there again, we'll have no choice but to call the police."

I don't fucking care. They can throw me in jail if they want. My asshole grandfather will just bail me out. He's going to force me to do his bidding until his dying gasp.

But the guy in scrubs was right about one thing. My getting in the doctors' way isn't going to help my mother. I finally let out a breath and move a few seats down in the waiting room, getting as close to the double doors as I can. The magazines on the table next to me are wrinkled and outdated.

Doesn't anyone ever think to update the magazines in a hospital waiting room?

It's always like this. Always.

Five minutes go by.

Then ten.

And all I can think about is my mother lying dead on the table. Without Dad. Without me. Without Savannah. Without anyone to hold her hand and give her comfort. Tell her that she's loved.

I stand, pace around the waiting room, running my fingers through my hair.

Please.

I can't lose my mother.

Then I laugh at myself. Hell, I went seventeen years without seeing her. Without seeing my father. Without having any contact with either of them.

I walked away from all of this. Perhaps this is my punishment now.

But if there's a God in heaven, He ought to know I'm trying to do the right thing. Sure, I arranged Puzo's death, but he was a derelict, a guy who deserved to die. I have to look at the bigger picture here.

The bigger picture of...

Shit. Puzo had kids.

Maybe he was a bad man, but he had two kids. Raven's friend was their nanny.

And I took their father away from them.

And now maybe it's only fair for *me* to lose a parent as well.

An eye for an eye.

But even if *I* deserve this, Savannah doesn't deserve to lose her mother. My father doesn't deserve to lose his wife.

Fuck. I've got to get out of here.

I'm going to go slowly crazy—

"Anyone here for Caroline Gallo?"

I jerk and turn toward the sound of the man's voice. He stands by the double doors.

I stride quickly toward him. "I'm her son. Vincent Gallo."

"Mr. Gallo, I'm Dr. Fife." He shakes my hand. "We've been able to get your mother stabilized, but she's going to need a triple bypass surgery."

"So she's not... I saw the paddles..."

He nods. "Yes, her heart did stop, but we were able to get it going again. We're going to keep her under observation, and if she remains stable, we'll be operating on her first thing in the morning."

"How did my mother have a heart attack? She's active, and she eats right."

But does she? She and Dad always ate a lot of pasta and cheese.

"Heart issues in women are more common than most people think," he says. "In the meantime, she was asking for her husband. Is he here?"

Nope. He's locked up. "He can't be here at the moment. May I see her?"

"Yes. I'll take you back. We'll be moving her to the ICU as soon as we can."

I hold myself steady as I follow the doctor back.

My mother is still hooked up to all kinds of machines, and her eyes are closed.

"She needs her rest," the doctor says. "Like I said, we'll be transferring her up to the ICU as soon as we get a bed ready."

I swallow and nod. "Thank you. Thank you for saving her."

"She's strong. She should recover well after surgery." He gives me a smile—I can't tell if it's forced or not—and turns to the door. "I'll give you a moment." He whisks out of the area.

"Mom?" I say gently, tugging on her arm.

Her eyes open. "Vinnie? Savannah?"

Crap. I haven't called Savannah. "She'll be here as soon as she can, Mom."

"What about your father?" She blinks heavily. "I need to see...my husband."

She is delirious.

"You know he can't be here, Mom. He's..."

"Yes, I know." Her eyes close again.

There's not much else I can say to her, so I'll let her rest.

I'll stay with her until they get her transferred up to the ICU, and of course I'll be back for her surgery in the morning.

In the meantime, I have to call my grandfather. Tell him I didn't get on that plane.

Not looking forward to that one. I punch in his number and hold the phone to my ear.

"Shouldn't you be airborne about now?" his voice says.

"Hello to you too."

"That's not funny, Vincent. What the hell is going on?"

"You may have to take care of this Colombia thing yourself. My mother—your daughter—has had a heart attack."

No response.

Not that I expected one. Why should he care? It's only his daughter. His only child.

"You have anything to say, old man?"

His voice is steady. "Where is she? What hospital?"

I relay the information.

"I'll be there right away."

I don't particularly want to see him, but so be it. She *is* his daughter. If he wants to see her—which I doubt; I'm sure he has some ulterior motive for coming—I won't stop him.

A few orderlies enter the curtained-off area. "We're going to take Mrs. Gallo to the ICU now," one of them says.

"Thank you. I'm her son. I'll be coming along."

"Of course. We found a private room, and you're welcome to stay with her if you'd like."

Perhaps I should. But she's in good hands.

Several minutes later, when they've got my mother transferred and hooked up to all the machines in the ICU room, I finally call Savannah.

"Vinnie?" Her voice is hoarse. I probably woke her up. "Is everything all right? It's awfully late to be calling."

"Don't freak out, Sav, because she's going to be all right, but Mom had a heart attack this evening."

She gasps, and I hear the phone clatter to the floor.

"Vinnie?" Falcon's voice.

"Is she okay?"

"She's in shock, I think. What happened?"

"Our mother had a heart attack. They had to revive her with the paddles. But they got her back. She's scheduled to have a triple bypass in the morning."

"Oh my God. We'll be there right away. What hospital?"

"Just be here for the surgery in the morning. It's scheduled for 9 a.m. You guys don't have to come now."

"I don't think I can keep Savannah away."

"All right. Have it your way. But she is in the ICU. I don't know if they limit the number of people we can have in the room with her. I'll have to check."

"All right. We're on the way. Call us when you know."

"Of course. I'll step out if I must to let Savannah have some time with Mom."

"Of course. And Vinnie?"

"Yeah?"

"You and I need to have a talk."

~

MY GRANDFATHER DOESN'T SHOW up. Big surprise.

But two hours later, Savannah, in tears, sits with our mother.

And I follow Falcon out into the hallway.

"We need someplace private," he says.

"There's an alcove at the end of the hallway on the other side from the elevators. With vending machines and all."

"It's late enough that we can probably be alone there," he says.

I lead him to the alcove, take a seat, and gesture for him to sit down across from me.

"What is it?" I ask.

He frowns. "Raven came clean."

"About what?"

"About the two of you, Vinnie."

I try to read Falcon's expression. He doesn't look angry. He doesn't look anything. Maybe he's worried about his future mother-in-law. About his fiancée.

I'm not sure what to think.

"And?" I prod.

"And you already know what I'm going to say." He takes a deep breath and looks me dead in the eye. "Right now…you're not good for her, Vinnie."

I let out an exasperated huff. "You think that's something I don't know? Look, I didn't plan what happened between Raven and me. And as her big brother, you have every right to pummel me. Though I could do the same to you for my little sister."

He doesn't react.

Not that I expect him to.

"I understand." He lets out a humorless chuckle. "And yeah, I kind of *do* want to pummel you. And believe me, I see the irony of the situation. But this isn't about me wanting to protect my baby sister's virginity." He sighs. "I'm more concerned about Raven's safety. She just got her life back, man."

"At the risk of repeating myself, do you think that's something I don't know?"

He crosses his arms. "I just don't know what you were thinking."

"Thinking had nothing to do with it, on either of our parts. We both knew what we were getting into. She did as well as I did. She's a grown woman, Falcon."

"She is." He casts his gaze to the hospital tiles. "I just... I need you to understand that I can't imagine life without her. I already lost out on so much time when I was in the clink. And when she got sick, she had to start missing visitation as well. Do you know how that felt, Vinnie? To know my sister was literally dying, and there was nothing I could do?"

"You ended up doing more than anyone else."

"You're right. By some miracle, *my* bone marrow was a match for her. Over her *twin* sister. But that's not even what I mean. They put her through so much chemo and radiation before they even considered the bone marrow transplant. Apparently her type of leukemia normally responds to traditional treatment better than bone marrow. I was a last resort, and thank God it worked, but she went through *years* of misery before that. And now that she's got a second chance at living a normal, happy life, you come waltzing in with another series of threats to her wellbeing." He closes his eyes and rubs at his temples. "The least you could have done was keep it in your pants."

I poke him in the shoulder. "May I remind you that the only reason I returned to the States was to help *your* fiancée avoid marrying Miles McAllister. The only reason I met Raven was because I was trying to help my sister." I sigh and lean away from Falcon. "I didn't mean for anything to happen, Falcon. But you know just as well as I do that sometimes you can't control how two people feel about each other."

Falcon scratches the back of his neck. "Well, when you put it that way..."

I hold up a hand. "And I get what you're trying to say. That you were behind bars and couldn't protect her. But Falcon, there wasn't anything you could've protected her from. Her illness... There was no way to reason with it. Beating it to death wouldn't have helped. Trying to get it to see logic wouldn't have helped."

He rakes his fingers through his hair. "I know that. But still, I couldn't be with her. Couldn't come to her, comfort her..." He shuts his mouth.

"Protect her?"

He nods.

"Funny that I knew exactly what you were going to say. But didn't we just have this discussion? You couldn't have protected her from the illness."

He narrows his gaze. "But the illness isn't the problem anymore. I *can* protect her from you, Vinnie. From the life you lead."

I hold up my hands. "Falcon, there's nothing I'd like more than to protect her from myself. I mean her no harm, of course. I love her. I am completely and totally in love with her. Hopelessly in love with her. And because I love her, I'm trying to walk away."

His eyes go wide.

"I've told her as much. In no uncertain terms. Apparently she hasn't let you in on that."

"No." He meets my gaze. "But thank you."

"I want you to think about something, though. Would you be able to leave Savannah? If it meant keeping her safe?"

"Christ, Gallo." He closes his eyes, inhales slowly. "It would be the hardest thing I've ever done, but yes, I could do it."

"Then you understand my feelings." I stand, pace around the area. "I've done a lot in my life. And a lot of it was very difficult." I stop and turn toward Falcon. "But nothing is more difficult than walking away from your sister, Falcon. Walking away from what may be my one great love. But I'll do it. And I'll do it gladly. Well, maybe not *gladly*. But I'll do anything to keep her safe, even if it means letting her go."

He sighs. "You're a good man, Vinnie."

I look down. "You wouldn't say that if you knew everything I've done."

"You don't know everything *I've* done either," Falcon says. "On the inside, you do what you have to in order to protect yourself. To protect your allies. Your cellmates. It wasn't all pretty." He takes another deep breath. "A lot of it I can't think about. But you think *I'm* a good man, don't you?"

"I wouldn't let you be with my sister otherwise," I say.

"And I wish I could let you be with mine." He frowns wistfully. "Maybe someday."

I nod.

But I know the truth.

Raven will never be safe with me.

I used to think that maybe once I take my grandfather down, there's hope for us to have a life together.

But now I can't push a nagging thought out of my head.

I'll do what has to be done. I'll put an end to the family.

But that may mean putting an end to myself as well.

23

RAVEN

When I wake up the next morning, it's time to tell my mother and father that I'm moving back to my own place.

I'm stunned when I find the police at our house, taking down the barriers to my room.

"What's going on?" I ask my father.

"The investigation is being closed. The police have gotten all the evidence they can, and it's not enough to continue," Dad says. "So you can have your room back, Raven."

I shake my head. "I don't want it back."

"I understand."

I fold my arms. "How can it no longer be a crime scene? A man was murdered here." I swallow down a fresh wave of nausea. "Or...murdered elsewhere and *placed* here."

Dad takes a deep breath and sighs it out. "As I've told you, the police have determined that none of us are suspects, and because there's no other evidence that they found in this room—fingerprints for anyone else—the investigation is currently closed."

I drop my jaw. "But someone *killed* him," I say. "How can they close the investigation?"

"Raven, this is a good thing for us. Trust me on that."

"But an innocent man is dead—" I stop abruptly.

He says nothing.

Oh my God.

"You don't think he *was* innocent, do you? You think Brick was involved in something..."

Dad looks down the hall. "I have no proof of anything, Raven. I don't plan to look for proof. But I can only repeat what I told you. The attorneys at his firm were looking for an excuse to get rid of him."

"They didn't have to have him killed."

"I don't for a moment think that his partners are behind this. But whoever did this to Latham did his firm a favor."

I gasp. "Daddy, I can't believe those words are coming out of your mouth. A man is dead. I thought he was a good man, and maybe I was wrong. But he didn't deserve to be killed. He didn't deserve to have his throat cut."

Dad frowns, scratches the side of his head. "You're right. He probably didn't."

"There's no *probably* about it. What happened to him was horrific."

Dad says nothing.

He's a powerful man in Texas. That much is sure. But he couldn't keep Falcon out of prison. He doesn't have the kind of power that Vinnie's grandfather has.

"I'm not moving back into my room, Daddy."

"I don't blame you. Go ahead and stay in the guestroom. We'll make that your room. We'll turn this one into... I don't know. More storage space or something."

"No. You don't understand. I'm not moving back into my room because I'm moving back to my place."

Dad widens his eyes. "Raven, you're not ready."

"Believe me, I'm more than ready. I've got a state-of-the-art security system and a bodyguard vetted by Falcon and Leif. You can meet him if you want. He's waiting in the SUV."

I expect my father to pounce on that, but he doesn't.

Just as I suspected. He already knows about Jared.

"Does this bodyguard know how to take care of you if you have a medical emergency?"

I smirk. "You and Mom don't know how to take care of me if I have a medical emergency. Neither does anyone on your staff." I wrinkle my forehead. "Come to think of it, isn't it weird that no one was home Friday night when Brick was killed? None of your staff?"

"It was a Friday night, Raven. They always have Friday nights off. Your mother explained all that to the authorities."

I don't press it further.

Brick is gone, and nothing I say can bring him back. I suppose I should be happy that the police have ceased their investigation of our family. Still, someone killed Brick, and if the police have dropped the case, I'll never know why.

Vinnie might be able to find out, but he's out of town for a month and doesn't want me to contact him.

I sigh. I know it's for my own safety.

I need to get on with my life. I'm moving back to my home, and I'm going to work doggedly at this foundation project. That and I'm going to concentrate on living my life to the fullest. Of course, living to the fullest would mean living with the man I love, but since that's not possible, I'm going to smell every flower I come across. Watch every sunset. And work hard at my foundation, so I can help other people like me—people who may not have my financial resources—to combat their illness.

I force myself to walk into my bedroom so I can pack up my things. I try not to look at the bed. The bloody sheets are long gone, stuffed in an evidence bag somewhere, along with the comforter and everything else that was on my bed.

It's bare now, only the mattress, with the bloodstain that soaked through.

I'm surprised they didn't take that into evidence, but I suppose they had enough of Brick's blood.

I avoid looking at the mattress as I get everything packed up into a couple of suitcases.

Jared is waiting in his SUV.

What a horrible job. Sitting around in a car. I should have invited him inside.

But he's getting paid through the roof for his services, so I suppose I shouldn't worry too much about him.

I'm ready to go when I hear a buzzing sound from my purse.

I open it up, and then I jerk and gasp.

The buzzing sound isn't coming from my regular phone, but from the burner phone that the Uber driver gave me. The same one I called Vinnie on…

I take a look at the text message.

Stay away from Gallo.

What?

Vinnie's out of town for the next month. What do they think I'm going to do? I don't even know where he jetted off to. Probably for the best. If I knew, I might try to go after him, text or no text. I assume they're talking about Vinnie. They can't be talking about Savannah, can they? Or Vinnie's father?

He's in prison, for goodness' sake.

I'm not sure who to ask about this. The person I would normally ask is Vinnie, but he's out of the country and basically told me not to contact him. I could ask Jared, but he's my bodyguard, not my private investigator.

I suppose Falcon is the best choice. I dial his number.

"Raven, everything okay?"

"Yeah. But I need to talk to you. Can I come over?"

He pauses a moment. "I'm actually in Austin."

"In Austin? What for?"

"Savannah's mother had a heart attack. She's in surgery right now having a triple bypass."

I throw my hand over my mouth. "Oh my God. Are you two all right? We've got to tell Vinnie. He's out of town."

"Actually, Ray, Vinnie's right here."

I nearly drop my phone. "So he didn't get on that plane."

"I didn't know he was supposed to be on a plane. But no, he's here. Ray, you've got to—"

"Don't start telling me to stay away from him right now. He needs me. I'm on my way. Which hospital?"

"Ray..."

"You can tell me, or I can have Jared drive me to every hospital in Austin, Falcon. Telling me will make it easier on both of us."

He sighs. "Austin General."

"See you soon." I end the call, grab all my suitcases, and walk out the door.

Jared helps me load them up. "You ready to go home, Raven?"

"No, Jared. We're going to Austin. Austin General Hospital. And step on it."

24

VINNIE

Before Michael and Savannah came along, it was just me and Mom. Those were the days I remember best, the days when it felt like we were a team, just the two of us against the world. Dad was hardly ever home.

I woke up every morning to the smell of coffee and the sound of Mom humming in the kitchen. She had—still has—a soft voice, the kind that wraps around you like a warm blanket. I would always find her standing by the stove instructing the cook about what to make for breakfast.

"Morning, sweetie," she'd say.

I'd run up to her, hugging her around the waist, and she'd lift me into her arms and set me on her hip. I'd eat my pancakes—my favorite—and then I'd give her a sticky maple-syrup kiss on her cheek.

After breakfast, we'd head out for our daily adventures. Mom would take me to the park, where we'd spend hours playing. I'd climb the jungle gym while she watched, her eyes never leaving me. She'd cheer every time I made it to the top, clapping her hands and calling me her little champion. We'd sit on the bench afterward and share a chocolate chip cookie.

Our afternoons were filled with stories. We had this giant recliner, and I'd curl up next to her with my head on her lap. She'd read to me, her voice taking on different characters, bringing each story to life. Sometimes, she'd make up stories, weaving tales of dragons and knights, always making me the hero who saved the day.

On rainy days, we'd build forts out of blankets and pillows in the living room. Mom would crawl in with me, and we'd pretend it was our castle. We'd spend hours in there, playing games, drawing pictures, and just being together. She'd always make me feel like the king of our little world.

At night, Mom would tuck me into bed, kissing my forehead and whispering goodnight. She'd leave the door ajar, letting a sliver of light in from the hallway. I'd fall asleep to the sound of her softly humming. I felt safe and loved.

Those days with Mom were my favorite. Later, after Mikey and Savannah were born, I'd get a nanny, but before then, Mom and I had our own little bubble, a world where it was just us. Those memories of just me and Mom are the ones I hold closest to my heart. They're the ones that remind me of how special our bond is, even as our family grew.

One time, when I was about thirteen years old, after Michael and Savannah had come along, Mom admitted to me that I was her favorite.

I was shocked, to be honest. She and Savannah seemed to have a special bond. They would do their mother-daughter things that Mikey and I weren't part of. Not that we wanted to be a part of them.

But once Mikey came along, the bubble that Mom and I

had seemed to burst. He was a particularly cranky baby, and he took up a lot of her time. I started spending more and more time with the nanny, and as I got older, my father.

Looking back, I realize that he was beginning to groom me for work with the family.

Savannah was a good baby. And such a cutie, with chubby cheeks and a perpetual smile on her face.

I always thought she was Mom's favorite.

But one day when I was home from school sick, Mom told me I was.

I remember lying on the couch, wrapped in a blanket, my head pounding and my throat sore. Mom brought me a bowl of chicken soup, just the way I liked it, with extra noodles and a dash of pepper. She sat down next to me and brushed my hair back from my forehead.

"You know, you've always been special to me," she said softly.

I looked up at her, confused. "What do you mean, Mom?"

She smiled, a bit wistfully. "You were my first. The one who made me a mother. We had so much time together, just you and me. Those memories are precious to me."

"But what about Savannah?" I asked, my voice a little hoarse. "You two are so close."

"We are," she admitted. "And I love her dearly. But that doesn't change how I feel about you. You and I have a bond that's different. Unique."

I stared at her, processing her words. "So, I'm your favorite?"

She laughed softly and then looked me directly in the eyes. "Yes, Vinnie. You're my favorite. But if you say those words to your brother or your sister, I will deny them."

It felt like a secret, something just between us. In that moment, despite the ache in my head and the sickness in my stomach, a warmth spread through me. It was like a piece of that old bubble was still there, just for us.

From that day on, whenever I saw Mom with Savannah or taking care of Mikey, I remembered her words. It didn't matter if we didn't have as much time alone anymore. That special bond we had, the one we built when it was just the two of us, was still there, strong and unbreakable.

And every time I saw that twinkle in her eye when she looked at me, I knew she remembered too. Even when she was busy with my siblings, even when life got chaotic, I knew I held a special place in her heart.

It gave me strength, knowing that no matter what happened, no matter how much things changed, I would always be her favorite. That was enough to carry me through the toughest of times.

And times *were* tough. Leaving my mother and my siblings was one of the hardest things I've ever done. I never should have left. I missed seventeen years with my mother... and now she's lying on an operating table, her chest split open, with doctors cutting at her heart.

I sit in the sterile waiting room, the harsh fluorescent lights making everything look even colder than it already feels. My legs are bouncing up and down, a nervous habit I can't seem to control right now. I stare at the wall, trying to make sense of everything. It's been hours, and each tick of the clock feels like a hammer striking my chest.

When Mom told me I was her favorite, it felt like she gave me a piece of her heart to hold on to, something just for us. And now, that heart is on the line, fragile and exposed.

I think back to the times I spent with Dad, learning the ropes of the family business. Those moments were supposed to prepare me for the future, but now they just feel like a distraction from what really matters. I remember the nights spent in the study, Dad teaching me about deals and negotiations while Mom was upstairs with Mikey, trying to soothe him. It felt like I was being pulled in two directions, my heart torn between my responsibilities and my longing for those simpler times with Mom.

The waiting room is filled with other anxious faces, each person wrapped in their own worries, their own fears. I feel so alone, even though we're all here together. Savannah's head is on Falcon's shoulder, and I can see he's whispering soothing words to her. The nurses at the desk murmur softly to each other, occasionally glancing our way with sympathetic eyes.

I close my eyes and try to focus on my breathing, but all I can think about is the way Mom used to sing to me when I was little. Her voice was soft and sweet, a lullaby that could chase away any nightmare. I wish she could sing to me now, tell me that everything will be okay.

Time is suspended. An hour could have passed, or a day. I rub at the headache behind my eyes when—

"Mr. Gallo? Ms. Gallo?"

I jerk abruptly into a stand. "Yes? How is our mother?"

The doctor—I don't remember his name—smiles. "She's stable. The surgery went well. She's in recovery now, and you'll be able to see her soon."

Relief floods through me, and my knees go weak. I sink back into the chair. Savannah weeps in Falcon's arms.

"Thank you, Doctor," Falcon says. "Thank you so much."

As I wait for the moment I can see her, I hold onto the hope that Mom and I will have more time together. More moments, more memories, more love. Because no matter what happens, I'll always be her favorite, and she'll always be mine.

25

RAVEN

I jump out of the car and run into the hospital, leaving Jared. He'll follow me, I'm sure, but at the moment all I can think about is Vinnie. How he needs me.

"May I help you?" the volunteer manning the reception desk asks.

"Caroline Gallo? She's having bypass surgery."

"Are you family?"

Am I? Technically, I guess so. "Yes. She's my brother's mother-in-law." Or she will be, once Falcon and Savannah get married.

That must be good enough, because she looks at her computer screen. "She's out of surgery but still in recovery. Your brother is probably in the waiting area on the second floor. You can—"

I stop listening and race toward the elevators. I've been to this hospital before. It's not where I had most of my leukemia treatment, but I had some tests done here. I know my way around.

By the time I reach the elevators, Jared has caught up to me.

Of course he has. He's being paid handsomely to be my bodyguard.

I don't speak.

He doesn't speak.

He knows why I'm here, and God bless him, he's not asking questions.

Good. His only job is to follow me and ensure my safety. Knowing the inner workings of my heart isn't part of his contracted obligations.

We get to the floor, and I read the signs that show me to the waiting area.

And there he is.

Vinnie.

His eyes are sunken and sad, his hair mussed, his suit rumpled. He's probably been here all night. Falcon and Savannah are there as well.

"Vinnie!" I rush toward him.

He widens his eyes slowly as he sees me. At first he doesn't move, but then he snaps to his feet, grabbing onto me. "Raven, my God. You shouldn't be here."

"Where else would I be? Your mother is having surgery."

"But—"

I take his face in my hands. "I know all the 'buts,' Vinnie. Why we can't be together. Why you're no good for me. Right now I don't care. I love you, and my place is here at your side in this time of crisis. Is your mother okay? I heard she's out of surgery."

He blinks. "She's stable. Yeah."

"What can I do for you? A drink? Coffee?"

He grabs my hand and ushers me out of earshot of Falcon and Savannah. "You need to go, Raven." Then he looks up at Jared—my bodyguard the size of a tank—and raises his eyebrows.

"Falcon hired him," I say.

"Good. I need you to go. You're not safe with me."

"We're in a hospital, Vinnie. Nothing will happen to me here." I sigh as I realize what I just said. "That's a lie if I ever heard one. A hospital is where I found out I was sick. Where they pumped poison into my veins, and it didn't even kill the cancer raging inside me. God, I hate hospitals."

"Which is another reason why you shouldn't be here." He gives me a gentle push away from him. "Live your life, Raven. Please. I need you safe. I need to know you're happy."

"I'll be happy," I whisper, "as long as I'm with you."

"Fuck." He rubs his forehead. "You're killing me here." He grabs my hand and leads me down a hallway, checking doors.

We end up in a janitorial closet, the smell of cleaning products sharp in the air. He closes the door behind us and flips on the light. It feels cramped, but in this moment, I welcome the closeness.

"Raven," he starts, his voice rough. "I can't do that to you. I can't let you suffer because of me."

"But I *am* suffering, Vinnie," I say, my voice breaking. "Every day away from you is agony."

He runs a hand through his hair. "It's not about just you and me anymore," he says quietly. "You know that. It's about something so much bigger."

"I—"

But I stop talking when his mouth comes down on mine.

The kiss is raw and passionate, and I return it with all the love I feel for him.

I know what he's doing.

It's an escape mechanism. He was faced with his mother's mortality, and now he wants to feel his own life. His own heart beating.

After a moment, he pulls back, looking into my eyes, his own dark orbs overflowing with a million unspoken words. He cups my face, the rough pads of his thumbs catching on my cheeks. "I don't want you to get hurt, Raven. I can't bear the thought."

"But Vinnie," I plead. "We need each other. More than ever."

He lets out a long sigh and then his face softens. He pulls me against him, wrapping his arms tightly around me.

"I know," he says quietly after a few moments. "But I have to protect you...even from myself."

"We'll figure this out." I nestle closer to his chest, inhaling the familiar scent of him—a mixture of fresh air and spice.

Jared is likely listening right outside the door, but I don't care.

Honestly, it wouldn't kill us to have someone keeping a lookout for janitors or other hospital staff that might come into this closet.

Vinnie slides his fingers over my fuzzy head. "It can't be figured out. Don't you get it? I've done things. Terrible things. Things I can't ever take back. Hell, I don't even want to take them back. My life is going to get volatile. It's already volatile. I have a duty to Savannah, to my mother, to the memory of my brother. I have to—"

I place my fingers over his lips. "Right now, Vinnie, all you have to do is fuck me. Use me. Right here in this closet. Take me like we're animals. Do it. I need it as much as you do."

Vinnie's eyes darken. Without a word, he yanks me toward him, pressing his body against mine, and he kisses me. I return the kiss and tangle my fingers in his gorgeous hair.

He breaks the kiss and pulls away. I whimper at the loss.

"Raven... Are you sure?"

Instead of answering, I reach up to pull him back down to me. Our lips connect in another hard kiss and I feel his hesitation melt away. A low growl escapes him as he tightens his grip around my waist.

The world outside blurs away as we lose ourselves in each other. The cold linoleum floor beneath us, the smell of bleach and soap—none of it matters. All that matters is him and me. This moment. Here, the chaos from the outside world can't touch us, can't interfere with what we have.

Vinnie runs his hands up my back, his touch electrifying as he grinds against me, his need evident even through the layers of clothing between us. He pulls at my shirt, breaking away from our kiss just long enough to slide it over my head.

I let out a loud moan and arch into him, clutching at his hair. His hands are everywhere, making me feel alive. Tangled with each other amidst brooms and buckets seems symbolic of our lives—chaotic and messy.

Yet it feels so right.

"Raven," he whispers again, his voice low and husky.

The sound of my name on his lips strikes me somewhere deep within.

Without further words, he helps me out of my sweats and

then he unbuckles his belt and unzips his fly. He lifts me onto a metal shelf, and I wrap my legs around him.

In a moment, we're lost in each other. He's inside me, thrusting, thrusting, thrusting...

Completing me in the way only he can.

Finding solace and escape in the midst of the storm brewing outside.

With each movement of him inside me, I come close to the peak, and when he releases inside me, I join him in climax. When the pulsing subsides, our bodies are intertwined, my head resting on his chest as I listen to the steady rhythm of his heart.

He trails his fingers lightly over my scalp, sending shivers down my spine.

"I wish things were different," he murmurs, his voice barely above a whisper as he traces my cheekbone.

"I know," I reply softly.

A sigh ripples through him, and he pulls me tighter. He doesn't speak again for a while, the silence broken only by the steady thrumming of his heartbeat and the distant hum of hospital life outside the door.

Eventually, I shift in his arms, reluctantly beginning to pull away. But he tightens his grip on me, his gaze intense. "Stay," he says simply. It's not a command, but a desperate plea.

"Vinnie—"

"I need you here, Raven. Just for a little while longer."

His voice is laced with an emotion so raw and real that it nearly shatters my heart. I can't refuse him. Not when he looks at me like that—as if I'm his lifeline.

I nestle back into the warmth of his embrace, letting the

rhythmic beating of his heart lull me into a sense of peace and comfort. We stay huddled together in the small closet for what feels like hours, sharing in each other's warmth and stealing moments of tranquility amidst the chaos outside.

"We should probably get back," I finally whisper.

Vinnie's grip tightens momentarily before he releases me, his fingers lingering on my skin.

"Let's fight this together," I say. "Let me help you."

He looks to the ground and sighs. "No one can help me, Raven."

Those are his last words to me. He turns and opens the door to the closet.

And he runs right into Jared.

26

VINNIE

This dude is bigger than a pro linebacker. Damn.

He looks at me like he wants to tear me in half, and I'm betting he could. I'm a tall and broad guy, but I'm dwarfed in comparison to this man. He's several inches taller than I am, and he must live in the gym, based on how big the muscles on his shoulders and chest are.

But he doesn't touch me.

He simply looks at Raven. "You okay?"

She nods. "I'm fine. Thank you for not...interrupting."

I walk around Jared.

Raven follows me. "Vinnie..."

"I have to get back. My mom will be coming out of recovery soon, and—"

"And I'll be right beside you when she does, no matter who tries to tell me not to be."

I cock my head. "What do you mean? I'm the only one who's told you to stay away. And you've made it clear that you won't."

She pulls out her phone and shows me a text.

Stay away from Gallo.

My heart pumps directly into my throat when I see the words. "Fuck," I mutter.

"Do you know who sent this?"

"Who do you think? My grandfather, most likely." I lower my voice. "You should take the advice."

"No." She grabs my arm, squeezes my bicep. "I know how much your mother means to you, Vinnie. I won't leave you alone."

She's so damned stubborn. Hers is the kind of persistence that wins wars. And right now, she's the kind of woman who isn't going to let a mob boss's threats keep her from standing by my side in my time of need.

I look at Raven, really look at her, and find a strength within those dark eyes that both frightens me and ignites a spark within me.

I gently brush her hand off my arm. "I can handle this. You don't need to put yourself in danger for me."

"It's not about what I need," she replies, tucking her phone back into her pocket. "It's about what *you* need."

"You're impossible," I mutter, rubbing my temples as if that could somehow rub away the inevitable headache this situation was bound to cause.

"I prefer 'relentless.'" She smiles. "You don't have to do this alone."

Before I can respond, her phone chimes with another text. Her face hardens as she reads it. Then she turns the screen to show me.

Stay away from Gallo. This is your last warning.

"Fuck," I mutter.

"We'll work this out," she says softly.

"We?" I grab her shoulders forcefully. "There is no 'we' in this, Raven. This is my life, my family, my problem."

Her dark eyes don't flicker in the face of my outburst. Instead, they harden as if cast from steel. "Your life became *our* life when you told me you love me. I'm not backing down now."

I gape at her, momentarily struck dumb by the steel in her voice. Then, with a deep breath, I compose myself, letting go of her shoulders. "Raven, you don't understand. My grandfather is dangerous. He doesn't make idle threats."

"He's not the only one who can be dangerous, Vinnie." She crosses her arms defiantly. "I'm not one to be scared off by threats."

I swallow. "And what if he decides to make his point a little clearer next time? What if he tries to hurt you?"

"We'll face this together, Vinnie." She places a hand on my cheek. "That's what people who love each other do."

"We're not normal people, Raven," I reply bitterly, "and this isn't a normal situation."

"No," she agrees. "But we are two people who care for each other deeply. And I swear to you —"

"Vinnie!"

I look up to see Savannah rushing toward us.

My heart races again. Something must have happened.

"Is she okay?"

Savannah grabs my hands. "Thank God I found you. Yes, Mom's out of recovery. She's been transferred to her room in ICU, and we can see her now."

I wrangle out of Raven's grasp. I look deep into her eyes. "Please go home. I don't want you here." Then I turn, unable to look at the sadness that is no doubt covering her face at my words.

Savannah's jaw drops, but she says nothing, simply leads me back.

"Have you seen her?" I ask Savannah.

"No, not yet. The doctor says you and I can go in together."

"All right."

She nudges my arm. "Vinnie..."

I shake my head. "I can't talk about that. I absolutely can't. So don't ask."

Savannah gulps and simply nods.

We find a nurse who leads us back into the ICU wing into our mother's room.

"She's still asleep," the nurse says. "But her vitals look good for now. She may be out for another couple of hours. Even after that, she's going to be groggy."

"The drugs last that long?" Savannah asks.

"Not so much the drugs. Although yes, they will make her groggy for the next twenty-four hours or so. But remember that sleep is the way the body heals. This has been traumatic on her body. She's had her chest cut open, her sternum cracked and split, her heart—"

"Please," Savannah interrupts. "We know the details. We don't need to hear them again. It's just so difficult to think of my mother that way."

The nurse nods. "I understand. But please don't hesitate to ask if you have any questions."

"We won't," I assure her.

"I'll give you some privacy then. I can only let you stay for a few moments. Like I said, she's asleep, but she will probably be able to sense your presence. Feel free to talk to her. Reassure her that you're here and that everything's okay."

Once the nurse leaves, Savannah turns to me. "You should go first, Vinnie."

"Why me?"

She scratches her arm. "Because we both know how Mom feels about me at the moment. She's not my biggest fan."

I lay a hand on her shoulder. "Sav, she nearly died. However she was feeling about you has no bearing now. She's alive, and she loves you. In fact, I was just thinking about how close you two were when you were a kid. How she would take you to do mother-daughter things."

Savannah smiles at that. "Yeah. I remember this one picnic..." She shakes her head. "She was a good mother, Vinnie. Or she tried to be, anyway."

"She was resigned to her place in the world. In the family," I say. "I think part of her problem with you is sheer jealousy, Sav. You're getting to live the life she didn't get to live. A life on your own terms, with the man you chose, not one who was chosen for you."

"Yeah, I get that, but shouldn't she be happy for me? I'm her kid."

I take in a deep breath, closing my eyes and running my hands through my hair. "I think in her own way she is. She just feels... I guess she feels like I came back for you. And she was just as happy to have me overseas. Where I was safe from our grandfather."

"I'm not sure that's the case."

The voice sends chills down my spine.

Savannah and I both turn around. Our grandfather

stands in the doorway. He takes a few slow steps into the room.

"And how is my daughter?" he asks, his voice solemn.

"You'd know if you bothered to come last night like you said you would," I say to him.

He snaps his head in my direction. "Watch your tone with me, Vincent. You expect to gain my trust by being belligerent?"

"I've done everything you asked," I say.

He leers at me. "If that were true, you'd be in Colombia."

"What are you talking about, Grandpa?" Savannah demands. "This is our mother. You really think Vinnie was going to get on a plane when our mother—"

"Be quiet, Savannah," Grandfather says. "When I want your opinion, I'll ask for it. And believe me, that day will never come."

Instinctively, my hands curl into fists. I could break the motherfucker's nose right now for talking to my sister that way.

But I hold myself in check.

"Sav," I say. "Excuse us for a moment. Spend some time with our mother."

I walk toward Grandfather, effectively pushing him out the door and closing it behind me. I walk with him to the alcove at the end of the floor.

"What the hell was that about?" I ask.

He scoffs. "What? About Savannah?"

"Of course not. I know *exactly* what that was about. I know how you feel about Savannah. You think of her as a second-class citizen, just the way you think of your own daughter. The woman who, by the way, gave you three grandchildren."

He exhales sharply out of his nose. "That's debatable."

I cock my head. Did he just say what I think he said?

"What the hell is that supposed to mean?"

He smirks. "Read into it whatever you want, Vincent."

"I can't say anything about myself, but I remember my mother being pregnant with Mikey and Savannah. I remember touching her belly and feeling the baby's kick. They are your grandchildren, Grandfather."

His face remains stoic. "Yes, they are."

What the hell is he trying to say?

I have no idea. But I *do* know what I need to get done.

"You need to stop texting Raven Bellamy."

"You are not in any position to tell me what to do."

I raise an eyebrow. "At least you're not denying it."

"Is that what you want? Fine. I haven't been texting Raven Bellamy." He scowls. "Why would I bother with Raven Bellamy? She's of no consequence to me at all."

I shake my head slowly. "That's where you're wrong. You know she means something to me, and you're not one to let any kind of potential leverage pass you by."

"She's better off if she stays the hell away from you, Vincent."

"Well, for once we agree on something." I shove my hands in my pockets. "Just leave her alone. I've ended it. All I want is for her to be safe."

"And she will be," he says, "as long as she doesn't interfere in things."

"She hasn't interfered in—" I stop.

We still don't know who that Uber driver who told her to invite me over last Friday night was...

Who...

Cogs start to turn in my head. Brick Latham was killed, and... Isn't it interesting that neither Raven nor her parents were home that night?

Perhaps my grandfather didn't have anything to do with the Uber thing after all.

Or...

"Did that attorney ever do any work for you?" I ask.

"What attorney?"

"The one whose throat was slit at the Bellamy ranch house Friday night," I say. "And don't pretend you don't know who I'm talking about. We've been through this."

"*That attorney* could mean anything, Vincent. I have many attorneys, and why on earth would I ever do business with an attorney who specializes in nonprofit organizations?"

"Why wouldn't you? Nonprofit organizations are a great way to launder money."

He presses his lips together, and I can see the tension in his face.

I'm on to something, and he knows it.

I point at him sharply. "Fuck it all. It *was* you."

"Vincent, I am never one to *not* own up to what he has done," he says. "And for once, it was not me."

"Then who?" I pace around him. "Who the hell would want to get rid of Brick Latham? And who would do it at the Bellamy Ranch?"

"Whoever it was made sure that Raven and her parents were gone." He takes a slow breath in and furrows his brow at me. "I'm surprised at you, Vincent. Think about it. Think about who might want to get rid of Latham, but who'd also want to keep the Bellamys safe."

He's right. My grandfather doesn't give a damn if the Bellamys are safe or not. He was going to let Miles McAllister shoot Falcon in cold blood, and he didn't blink when he told me to kill Raven.

So who *is* interested in keeping the Bellamys safe?

And who might see Brick Latham as a threat?

I mull it over for a few minutes. Raven. My grandfather. Brick Latham. Falcon and Savannah.

My parents.

Raven's parents.

Then a lightbulb.

The answer comes to me…and it's not pretty.

27

RAVEN

"Raven," Jared says to me, "we should get out of here."

"No," I say succinctly.

He lays a gentle hand on my shoulder. "But he said he doesn't want you here."

I swat it away. "He's saying it because he wants to keep me safe, Jared."

"Yes, and so do I. I'm being paid very well to keep you safe. And frankly, Vinnie Gallo was right. The farther away from him you are, the safer you are."

I shake my head. "He needs me, Jared."

"He needs you *safe*." He taps a fist against his chest. "I can keep you safe, but you're making my job a lot more difficult than it needs to be."

I let out a humorless chuckle. "You have to earn your keep, don't you?" I sit down in one of the uncomfortable chairs in the waiting area.

Jared reluctantly sits next to me. "They're probably going to be with their mother as long as they can," he says.

I don't answer. Instead, my gaze is drawn to an older man walking through the waiting area and checking in with reception.

Already I know who that man is.

Mario Bianchi. Vinnie's grandfather. The resemblance between them is uncanny. I feel like I'm looking at Vinnie in fifty years.

Same facial features, same muscular build, although Mr. Bianchi is a few inches shorter. Same thick hair, only his is silver.

Same olive complexion.

Same dark eyes—except where Vinnie's are kind and sparkling, Mr. Bianchi's show malevolence.

A moment later, a nurse comes and escorts Mr. Bianchi into the ICU hallway.

He must be going to see his daughter. Vinnie must be back there with her, along with Falcon and Savannah, unless they went somewhere.

"That's Mario Bianchi," I say to Jared.

He nods slowly. "I know who it is." He jumps to his feet. "I want to get you out of here now."

"No. I can't leave Vinnie."

"You have to. That man is dangerous."

I cross my legs. "I'm perfectly safe in a hospital waiting room."

"Any maniac can come in here with a gun and start shooting people," he says.

"That can happen anywhere. In any restaurant, any hotel lobby. It's not going to happen here. And if it does? Mario Bianchi won't have anything to do with it. He's smarter than that."

Jared lets out a breath but doesn't say anything.

A few moments later, Falcon enters the waiting area.

"Where have you been?" I ask.

"I went to get a bite to eat," he says. "What are you still doing here?"

"I'm not leaving him, Falcon."

Falcon turns his attention to Jared. "Why is she here again?"

"I'm not her keeper," he says. "I can't force her to leave."

"Well, *I* can." Falcon grabs my arm and pulls me out of my chair.

"Get your hands off me," I say, attempting to wriggle out of his grasp.

Jared rises. "You may be the one paying me, but you're not going to manhandle her."

Falcon shakes his head and lets me go. He rubs at his forehead. "I'm sorry, Ray. You too, Jared. I just need you to be far away from here. Savannah is my fiancée, so I have to be here. But Bianchi could show up at any time."

"He's already here," Jared says. "He went back to his daughter's room."

Falcon widens his eyes. "See what I mean?" He turns to Jared. "Why didn't you get her the hell out of here?"

"Because I can't make her obey me, Mr. Bellamy. I'm her bodyguard. It is my job to keep her safe wherever she goes. And right now, despite my fervent insistence to the contrary, she wants to stay here."

"Right," I say, trying to sound more confident that I am. Frankly this whole discussion is making me very uncomfortable.

Savannah comes out of the hallway then and Falcon goes

to her. "Vannah," I hear him say as he takes her into an embrace.

I walk up to them. "How is she?" I ask.

Savannah sighs. "The nurse claims she's fine, but she's still asleep. But that's not what I'm worried about at this point."

Falcon grabs her hands. "Your grandfather's here."

"Yeah." She swallows. "He and Vinnie are down the hall talking. The nurse came in and said I needed to leave, that my mother needs her rest. I don't know why I can't stay. It's not like I was keeping her from resting."

"If you want to be in there, Vannah, that's where you'll be. I'll take care of it."

"Right now I'm more concerned about Vinnie and my grandfather." Her face twists, and she reaches into her purse for a tissue. "God, sometimes I wish Vinnie were still in Europe. I missed him, but he left when I was ten. I got used to life without him. And now he's back, and I love him, but you know what?" She dabs at her eyes. "I don't really even *know* my older brother."

"I do," I say. "He's a good man, Savannah."

"Oh, Raven..." Savannah sighs. "There's still so much that you don't know."

Falcon turns his head sharply toward his fiancée. "And we're going to keep it that way."

"For your information, Savannah," I say, "I happen to be in love with your brother. And there's nothing that you can say that will change that."

Savannah looks at me, and just when I think she's not going to say a word, she finally opens her mouth, only to close it abruptly when Mario Bianchi returns.

The muscles in my jaw tense. Then my whole body tenses. He walks out—perfectly clad in a designer suit—and he looks first at Falcon and then at Savannah.

Finally, his gaze rests on me. I feel a cold chill run down my spine, my whole body erupting in goosebumps.

"Ms. Bellamy," he says to me, "I can see what my grandson sees in you. You are absolutely stunning."

Is he being facetious? I'm wearing baggy sweats and a tight tank top. Flip-flops on my feet, my toes unpainted.

And of course we all know what my head looks like.

But I can see the lecherous look in his cold, dark eyes. He means what he's saying. He's mentally undressing me as we speak.

I swallow down a fresh wave of nausea.

"Grandfather," Savannah says, "please..."

Mr. Bianchi holds up a hand. "Oh, I'm being serious, Savannah. Ms. Bellamy is as lovely as they come." He turns his gaze back to me. "And yes, I realize you have no hair. That your eyelashes and eyebrows are only beginning to grow back in. I can only imagine how beautiful you were before your illness."

Falcon steps in between the two of us. "What the fuck do you want?" he asks through gritted teeth.

Mr. Bianchi looks Falcon up and down, his expression unchanging. "You look as though you're healing well."

"No thanks to your goons," Falcon says. "But it was about five against one, and I was tied to a chair."

"Yeah, and thanks to you, my son-in-law's now in prison."

"Grandfather, please..." Savannah rubs her forehead.

"You should be thanking your brother, Savannah." He turns to Falcon. "And you too, for that matter."

"I think most of my thanks go to your son-in-law," Falcon says. "If not for him, I'd be a dead man."

"And the world might be a better place," Bianchi says.

Savannah's eyes widen, and my temper flares.

"What the fuck?" I say. "My brother is alive thanks to your son-in-law. And he's a better man than you'll ever be."

Bianchi scoffs. "He's an ex-con."

"And *you're* a current con!"

I take a few steps toward him, but Falcon gestures me to stop. "Don't stoke the fire, Ray," he says. "It's not worth it."

"Where's Vinnie?" I demand.

"He's with his lovely mother," Bianchi says. "And now, please excuse me. My work never seems to be done."

"Figuring out who to kill next," Falcon mutters.

If Bianchi hears him, he doesn't show it.

"I'm going to go find Vinnie," I say.

"If he's with his mother, Ray, let them have a minute," Falcon says.

I want to tell my brother to fuck off, but he's right. Vinnie needs this time with his mom.

"Is there anything you need, Vannah?"

"Yeah. I need to eat something," she says. "Have you eaten?"

"I grabbed a bite while you were in there," Falcon says. "Come on. Let's get you something to eat. Raven, you should come with us."

"I'm going to stay here and wait for Vinnie."

"Have it your way."

I nod, watch them leave, and then I walk back to Jared and take my seat next to him.

28

VINNIE

Five Years Earlier...

The guilt used to eat at me. Day after day it gnawed into my psyche. My nightmares were dominated by Misha's face, the look he gave me as the light faded from his eyes.

Until one day, I stumbled into a Buddhist temple in the heart of Kathmandu. The air inside was heavy with the scent of incense and the low, mesmerizing hum of monks in prayer. I was drawn to the calm, to the peace that seemed to radiate from the stone walls and intricate tapestries.

One of the monks, an elderly man with a face wrinkled like a dried riverbed, approached me immediately, his saffron robe swishing softly against the stone floor. He seemed to be able to read my mind. Or maybe he simply welcomed everyone who came to his temple.

"Come," he said, guiding me towards a secluded corner of the temple. There we sat, cross-legged on plush cushions. His gaze didn't waver from mine as he instructed me in the ways of meditation—breathing in, breathing out, focusing on nothing but the rhythm of life flowing in and out.

Days turned into weeks under his patient guidance. A diet of simple rice and lentils sustained me as I delved deeper into the ancient practice. Each morning we began before dawn, welcomed by the soft light filtering through the temple's stained-glass windows. The vibrant colors danced around us as we meditated to the backdrop of the city's awakening.

As the days waned and the nights befell Kathmandu, the monk and I continued our practices under the star-speckled sky. Sounds of the city slowly faded away, replaced by the soothing whispers of nature and the rhythmic drone of our own breaths. His teachings gradually seeped into my mind, calming the tempest within, layer by layer.

After several weeks of this strict regimen, I am finally beginning to feel at peace.

One morning, as we sit in quiet contemplation, an epiphany washes over me like a wave crashing against a distant shoreline. The guilt, once a constant companion, is now but a mere whisper in contrast to my newfound serenity. I realize that it has been my choice to carry it, to let it fester and dictate my actions.

"You have arrived at a fork in your path," the monk says. "One path carries forth the guilt, while the other brings the promise of release and forgiveness."

Patience settles over me as I consider his wisdom. The choice seems easier now with this newfound clarity—to continue my journey shackled by the guilt of leaving Mikey, probably causing his death. Of killing Misha in Bucharest.

As the weeks have folded into months, I've discovered a

tranquility within me I had not known before. Each moment becomes an opportunity for mindfulness, each breath a reminder of the beauty of existence.

My days continue, filled with meditation, introspection, and a tranquility that seems as perennial as the stone walls of the temple. The city of Kathmandu thrums around us, but inside our little haven, time seems to stand still.

Until the monk approaches me, a serious look on his wrinkled face.

He lays a hand on my shoulder. “These walls are for learning, contemplation, Vincent.”

I nod.

“You have learned, you have contemplated, but now...” His eyes shine with a mix of pride and urgency. “You stand at the precipice of transformation. You’ve reached the limits of what this place can offer you. I have given you all the wisdom I possess. It is time.” He gestures to the temple gates. “Go now, with the strength of your spirit. Embrace the unknown. Continue your journey, and live your life to its fullest potential.”

~

Present Day...

Turns out the guilt was never truly gone. It was just on sabbatical. And as for my fullest potential? I doubt the monk —whose name I never knew—would consider what I’m doing to be living to my fullest potential.

But it’s what I have to do.

Sometimes, you’re faced with a choice, and you choose protection of your loved ones.

Sometimes, you confront yourself and find that your morals aren't what you thought they were. You're more morally gray than you ever imagined.

And sometimes, when you listen to your intuition—and your grandfather—you find out things you don't want to know.

I need to speak to Austin Bellamy.

And I need to speak to him today.

29

RAVEN

Waiting is the worst.

I have new respect for my parents and brothers and sister. All the waiting they did when I was stuck in the hospital, whether it was in my room sitting with me or eating the crappy hospital food.

"I'm hungry," I tell Jared.

"Let's get you something to eat, then."

I bite my lip. "I was thinking maybe you could bring me something. Like a turkey sandwich. That sounds good."

"I'm afraid you don't understand how this works yet, Raven," he says. "I'm paid to protect you. Which means I don't leave you alone. I'm a bodyguard, not an errand boy."

I blink. "You really think I wouldn't be safe in a hospital waiting area?"

"*Especially* not in any kind of public area. There was no security at the entrance to this hospital. People can come in here with guns and pepper spray and anything else."

"But Jared, really? You think someone is going to try to harm me here?"

His gaze darkens as he stares me down. "Right now, Mario Bianchi is in this hospital, so there's no way I am leaving your side."

I rise. I have to admire his devotion to his duties. Or to his paycheck, whichever is guiding him. "Fine. Let's go get something to eat. But as long as Vinnie is here, I'm not leaving this hospital."

Jared rises. "Okay. Let's go to the cafeteria."

All eyes are on me—or maybe Jared, because he has such an imposing figure—as we walk to the elevator and go down to the first floor where the cafeteria is located.

We walk in, and I head straight to the sandwich section. I suppose I should ask Jared if he wants anything. Thank goodness I have a trust fund. It will take lots of money to feed him.

"May I help you?" The woman behind the sandwich counter asks.

"Yes, please. I'd like a deli turkey on rye with some avocado, please."

"Bacon on that?"

I stop myself from licking my lips. "Bacon? Of course."

"Coming right up." She turns to Jared. "And for you, sir?"

"Please," I say to him. "It's on me."

"I'll have the same," he says. "Side of fries."

"Coming right up."

She busies herself making our sandwiches, and when they're done, I place them on the tray. I head over to the drinks section. Of course the machines don't stock Orange Crush, and there isn't any in the refrigerated section either. I opt for a diet soda.

"What do you want to drink?" I ask Jared.

"Just water." He grabs a bottle from the refrigerated section.

We check out, and then I take the tray to one of the tables. I don't like being away from Vinnie in the waiting area, but I don't really want to take the food up there.

"Dig in," I say to Jared.

"Turkey's my favorite," he says.

I cock my head. "I'd have taken you for a beef kind of guy."

He chuckles. "Why? Because of my size? It may interest you to know that I don't eat red meat."

"And you're working for a bunch of beef ranchers? Isn't that ironic."

He shrugs. "I work for whoever pays me to work. I happen to believe in what I'm doing. I trust Phoenix, which means I trust your brother. If they say you need me, then you need me."

I want to roll my eyes, but I don't. The fact of the matter is that an attorney was found dead in my bed at my parents' house.

So yeah, having a bodyguard is good. Having top-notch security at my home is good.

I'll stop complaining about it. Jared is only doing his job.

"So no red meat," I say. "Why?"

"Believe it or not, I just don't like the taste."

"Really? You're not some health nut who says it's hard to digest?"

"Actually, if you're talking about what you find in the grocery store, red meat is probably better for you than turkey or chicken."

I widen my eyes. "You're kidding, right?"

"Nope. I've done the research. So trust me, if I liked the stuff, I'd be eating it."

"What kind of research have you done?"

"You grew up on a ranch, so you probably know about the bovine digestive system. The four stomachs."

"Well, yeah. Of course I know that."

"In the United States meat industry, they pump a lot of shit into the animals to get them fattened up and to keep them resistant to disease. A lot of it is detoxed out through their digestive systems before the meat gets to us. Can't say the same for chicken, pork, or turkey."

I press my lips together. "Wow. I never thought of it that way. I'm used to eating the beef from our own ranch, which is all grass fed, and of course we don't inject them with any of that crap anyway."

"I'm sure your beef is better than the grain-fed crap. But trust me. If I were interested in what was best for me, I'd be eating beef."

I nod, putting my sandwich down on my plate. "How can you not like the flavor of beef? It's so savory and just delicious."

"Yet here you are eating turkey."

I laugh lightly. "Because I'm used to grass-fed beef. The other stuff tastes like shit to me."

He shrugs. "Maybe I'll try your beef then."

"You really should. You might change your tune." I take a bite of my turkey sandwich.

Here I am talking to my beefy bodyguard about grass-fed beef. The bodyguard who's been hired because an assassin might be sent to take me out at any moment. All while my—should I call him my boyfriend?—is navigating both his mother's medical emergency and his family's mafia dealings. Oh, and I'm still in recovery from a deadly disease, and my brother is a recent parolee.

My life has become surreal.

It's been surreal for the past couple of years. For a while, I was convinced it was over.

And now that it's not? I have to rely on this piece of white meat-fed beef across from me to keep me safe.

What is wrong with this world?

We engage in a little small talk here and there, but for the most part we eat in silence.

I've found that Jared is fine with silence, which is great, because so am I.

He has a job to do. To protect me.

He doesn't have to talk to me.

And I'm okay with that.

Once we're done, we start walking back toward the elevator.

The elevator opens and—

"Vinnie!"

Vinnie stands there, still looking rumpled but luscious.

He blinks a few times, rubs his eyes. "Raven."

I run into the elevator and squeeze him around his waist. "You're not leaving, are you?"

He draws in a slow breath. "I have some business to attend to."

"Is your mother okay?"

"She's still asleep, but Falcon and Savannah are staying with her." He gently wriggles out of my grasp, his eyes darkening. "Plus my grandfather is still up there."

"Where are you going?"

He doesn't look at me. "I told you. Business. And no, you can't come along." He walks out of the elevator, not looking back. "Goodbye, Raven."

My heart shatters. He still wants nothing to do with me. I realize that it's out of concern for my safety. I'm not an idiot. But the animal part of my brain is still sad that I can't be with him, snuggle up in bed with him, enjoy a normal life together.

I take a step out of the elevator. I guess there's no reason to stay now. I'm here for Vinnie, and if he's not here...

I whip my hand into the elevator as the doors begin to close. I get back inside, and Jared follows me.

I'm not sure why I'm doing this, but my gut is telling me to stay in this hospital.

"Why are we still here, Raven?" Jared asks, giving voice to my thoughts. "Vinnie has left, and he's the only reason you were—"

"Because his grandfather is here," I say.

Jared's eyes widen. "You're not going near him."

I roll my eyes. "He's an old man, Jared."

"An old man who is responsible for God knows what."

"Yes," I say. "And he's the reason Vinnie can't be with me. I want to find out why."

30

VINNIE

I walk briskly to the parking lot where Fred is waiting in my car. Elmo is with him.

I need them both for what I'm about to do.

My heart dropped when I walked back out to the waiting area and found Raven and her bodyguard gone.

But I was also thankful. Seeing her would make it harder to do what I have to do.

And then of course... I had to see her when I came out of the elevator.

I should've known she wouldn't go quietly.

I looked back right as I was about to leave. I saw her getting back on the elevator.

My first instinct was to turn around and ask her why she wasn't leaving. After all, she told me the only reason she had come to the hospital was to be there for me.

So why is she going back up there? Maybe to check on Falcon? I don't know, and I can't take the time to dwell on it. Right now, I'm driving to the Bellamy Ranch.

I will talk to Austin Bellamy. And I will figure out what's going on.

~

FRED STEERS up the driveway into the Bellamy's large ranch house.

Everything looks the same as it did when I dropped Raven off here last week. No one can tell a crime was committed on these premises.

I don't trust my grandfather as far as I can throw him, but I believe him. My intuition tells me he had nothing to do with Brick Latham's murder.

And he's right about one thing. If someone got to Brick Latham, thinking they were getting to Raven...

None of it makes sense.

Except it does in a warped way.

I'm beginning to believe that Austin Bellamy is not the same man he's made out to be.

I get out of my car.

"Sir?" Elmo says.

I hold up a hand. "Stay here for now. I've got my phone. Be on alert. I'll let you know if I need you."

I walk to the door. Ring the bell.

A woman answers. "Yes, may I help you?"

"I'm here to see Mr. Bellamy."

She cocks her head. "Do you have an appointment with him?"

"I don't, but I think he'll see me." I hold out my hand and give her my card. "I'm Vincent Gallo Junior."

She reads the card, her forehead wrinkled. She looks

back into the house. "I'll need to check and see if he's in the house. Sometimes he's in the barns. But I know he's on property today."

"Good. Find him. I'm sure he'll see me."

"All right." She takes a few steps inside and gestures down the foyer. "Would you like to come in and wait in the living room?"

"Yes, that would be fine. Thank you."

She holds the door open for me and I walk in. The house is huge. A great big ranch house. Much different from my parents' home in Austin, though just as large.

She gestures to the living room. "Have a seat. Can I get you anything to drink?"

"I'm fine, but thank you for the offer."

The woman I recognize as Raven's mother walks in. She narrows her gaze when she sees me.

"Lucy, who is—"

"Mrs. Bellamy," Lucy, apparently, says. "This gentleman wants to see Mr. Bellamy."

"Whatever for?" She walks toward me and offers her hand. "I'm Star Bellamy."

Star Bellamy is a beautiful woman. Her skin is dark, about the same color as mine—different from Raven's fair skin. She must get that from her father. But the dark eyes, that mesmerizing, beautiful stare, she gets from the woman before me.

"I'm Vincent Gallo Junior," I say. "It's nice to meet you, Mrs. Bellamy."

"Oh?" Her eyes widen. "You're Savannah's brother."

"I am."

"I'm sorry." She presses her lips together, looking me up and down. "You don't look anything like Savannah."

"No. I look more like my mother. Savannah takes after our father."

"Well… Welcome to our home, Mr. Gallo."

"You can call me Vinnie, ma'am."

"Of course. Vinnie. Austin should be back soon."

"I'd like to wait, if possible. It's very important."

She parts her lips slightly. "Is… Is Raven all right?"

I nod quickly. "Yes, she's at the hospital. My mother… She had a heart attack yesterday."

"I'm so sorry. Is she all right?"

"She had a triple bypass this morning. She's out of recovery and has been moved to ICU. Falcon and Savannah are with her. And Raven is still there."

She places her hand over her heart. "My Raven… There never was a more caring soul. All that time she was sick and all she ever worried about was how the rest of us were coping."

"Yes, ma'am."

I'm not sure what else to say. I could tell her what a wonderful woman her daughter is, but she already knows that. What will it do to this poor woman when she finds out her husband may not be the pillar of society that the state of Texas seems to think he is?

But I can't concern myself with Mrs. Bellamy's feelings.

I need to make sure Raven is safe. That is, after all, why I told her we can't be together.

"Is this anything I can help you with?"

"I really do need to speak to your husband, if that can be arranged."

She looks out a nearby window onto the sprawling Bellamy property. "I'm expecting him back any minute. He went out to talk to a couple of the foremen this morning. But he's always back in time for lunch."

"All right. Thank you." I eye the room and head toward the most comfortable-looking couch. "I'll just have a seat here and wait for him."

"Don't be silly. You'll join us for lunch, of course." She turns back to Lucy. "Set another place in the kitchen, please."

"I don't want to impose."

"There's no imposition." She lays a delicate hand on my shoulder. "Please, join us."

"All right. I'll just sit here until you're ready."

She nods. "Lucy will come get you when lunch is served."

"Thank you again."

I sit down on the sofa in the elegant living room. A mahogany grand piano sits in the corner. It makes me think of Belinda.

What am I going to do about her?

I probably should've gone home to change. God only knows what I look like. I'm sure there are bags under the bags in my eyes. I haven't slept. And my suit is wrinkled.

Time seems to pass in a warp, and I'm pretty sure I slip somewhere into the gray area between consciousness and unconsciousness. I'm not sure whether seconds or hours have passed when Lucy comes in.

"Mr. Gallo, lunch is served."

"Thank you." I rise and follow her into the large gourmet kitchen, where three places are set.

"Mr. Bellamy is just washing up. He'll be here in a moment."

"Please, take the seat next to me," Mrs. Bellamy says. "It's nothing fancy today, I'm afraid. I hope you like hamburgers."

I chuckle. "I wasn't expecting lunch at all. And I love hamburgers. Thank you."

"What would you like to drink, Mr. Gallo?" Lucy asks.

I smile. "Do you have Orange Crush?"

Mrs. Bellamy smiles back. "That's Raven's favorite drink. We always have Orange Crush."

I stay standing until Mr. Bellamy arrives.

Austin Bellamy. I've seen pictures of him. But he's much larger in person. Tall and broad, with graying blond hair and piercing blue eyes. Fair skin, like Raven. But the rest of her looks she got from her mother.

"Mr. Gallo." He holds out his hand. "To what do we owe the pleasure?"

"I need an audience with you," I say.

"All right." He clears his throat. "Let's enjoy our lunch first, shall we?"

"Absolutely," I say with a smile. "I appreciate the invitation."

"Star always says everyone is welcome at our table." He gestures to my place. "Please, have a seat."

He holds out the chair for his wife.

I expected as much.

Austin Bellamy is known as a rancher and a gentleman. From what I can tell anyway. Since Savannah is marrying into the family, I've done my research.

Part of me hopes I'm wrong.

But part of me hopes I'm right.

Because if I'm not, someone else was behind the murder of that lawyer. And if it wasn't my grandfather...

Who the hell was it?

"We don't stand on ceremony at lunchtime," Mrs. Bellamy says. "Just help yourself. Guests first, of course."

"Obliged," I say. I grab a burger from the plate and place it on a bun. I add some lettuce, tomato, and just a tiny bit of onion. Then some ketchup and mustard.

I wait until Mr. and Mrs. Bellamy serve themselves, and then I take a bite.

"Delicious," I say after I wipe my mouth with my napkin.

"Bellamy beef. It's the best," Mr. Bellamy says.

"You might be right about that, sir."

He laughs. "Please, call me Austin."

"Of course. And you may call me Vinnie."

Austin takes another bite of his burger. "So, Vinnie. How are you finding the state of Texas now that you're home?"

"It's hot," I say.

Austin laughs. "It is that."

"When I left for Europe, our family was still living on Long Island. Texas is new to me. But I like what I see so far. It's a beautiful state."

"It is indeed. Everything is bigger and better in Texas, as they say." Austin takes a bite of his burger.

"Would you care for fruit salad, Vinnie?" Star hands me a crystal bowl filled with a mixture of cantaloupe, watermelon, grapes, raspberries, and blueberries.

"Thank you." I scoop some onto my plate and hand it to Austin.

"We can't thank you enough," Star says, "for what you've done for Falcon."

I resist the urge to lift my eyebrows. How much do they know about what Falcon went through at the hand of my family?

"All I need to know is that Savannah loves him," I say.

"Good man," Austin says.

I simply nod and take another bite of my burger.

Good man. Will he be saying the same after he and I have our talk?

I don't know that he will. I'm not sure what he thinks of me. He must know what my family does for a living.

Star chatters on and on about how well Raven is doing.

It's funny that neither of them bring up the fact that a dead body was found in their home only mere days ago. But I'll have plenty to say about that when I get Austin alone.

Once we're done with lunch, Lucy brings in dishes of simple vanilla ice cream for dessert.

"Star makes her own ice cream," Austin says. "There's nothing like it."

"I can't wait to try it then." I smile and take a spoonful of the ice cream.

Indeed, the ice cream is spectacular. So much creamier and with much more vanilla flavor than anything you can buy at the store. Even better than the gourmet ice cream Savannah served Raven and me at dinner last week.

"Wow," I say after swallowing. "This may be the best ice cream I've ever tasted."

"It's Raven's favorite," Star says. "She can't get enough of it."

"Just like her Orange Crush?" I can't help a smile.

"Exactly." Star smiles. "God broke the mold when he made that one."

I can't help grinning. "I can't disagree with that."

Once we're done with the ice cream and Lucy clears the

table, I turn to Austin. "Sir, if I may have a few minutes of your time in private?"

"Yes, of course." He rises. "Star, will you excuse us?"

"Yes, of course." She gets to her feet and collects the ice cream bowls. "You men go about your business. I'll just help Lucy clean up."

I follow Austin out of the kitchen and down a hallway to a large oak door. He opens it and gestures for me to go in.

He takes a seat behind the desk. "Please, have a seat."

I sit down in one of the plush leather chairs facing him.

"So, Vinnie, what can I help you with?"

I take a deep breath in and meet his gaze.

"You can tell me about Brick Latham."

31

RAVEN

Falcon joins Jared and me in the waiting area.

"Mr. Bianchi still in there?" I ask Falcon.

Falcon raises an eyebrow. "He's with his daughter and Savannah."

"Vinnie left," I say.

"He did?"

"Yeah. He said it was business. But if his grandfather is still here..."

Falcon shakes his head. "Anything can be business to those people."

"Vinnie is not one of *those people*," I say adamantly.

Falcon rubs at his forehead. "I agree with you, Ray. But right now... I don't want to even think about the kind of stuff he has to do."

"I prefer not to think of it either." I look over to Jared. "Could you excuse us for a minute? I want to talk to my brother alone."

Jared rises. "I can go stand there by the hallway, but my eyes will be on you the entire time."

"I understand."

Jared nods and walks out of earshot.

"He knows everything, Ray," Falcon says.

"He probably does. Sometimes I just want to talk to my big brother."

"I'm all ears. What do you want to talk about?"

I bite my lip. "First of all, how is Mrs. Gallo?"

"She's starting to come to, finally."

"Why did you leave Savannah in there alone with her grandfather?"

Falcon takes a slow breath in. "Actually, she asked me to. Trust me, it wasn't my idea. Savannah is kind of like you, Ray. She may look soft on the surface, but she's a spitfire. Even though you were a homebody and you'd rather be helping mom in the kitchen than be outside with Robbie, the boys, and me, you always had a feisty side."

"Falcon..."

"What?"

I lean in, my voice lowered. "I love Vinnie."

He smiles at me wistfully. "I know you do, Ray. I'd give you shit about it—about how you haven't known him long enough to be sure—but I can't. It was the same for Vannah and me."

I let out a short laugh. "Guess it's in the Bellamy DNA."

"One of the few perks that come with the namesake these days." Falcon looks down the hospital hallway. "Damn. I still can't believe what happened at Mom and Dad's house."

"Who do you suppose killed Mr. Latham?" I ask.

He frowns. "I wish I knew. I'd say Bianchi was behind it, but I can't believe he would do that to Savannah. Or even to

Vinnie. Let something like that happen on our property when he knows how much Savannah loves me."

"And how much Vinnie loves me?"

He frowns. "*Does* he know that, though?"

I scratch my arm. "Honestly, I have no idea. I believe Vinnie loves me. He's asked me in no uncertain terms to stay the hell away from him for my own protection."

"Which you should probably do, Ray."

I glare at him. "Would you be able to stay away from Savannah for your own protection?"

"No, but that's a little different." Falcon points to one of the many scars on his arm. "And besides, you see where that got me. If not for Savannah's dad, I'd be dead because I couldn't stay away from her."

"You weren't with her when you went barreling over to the Gallos'."

Falcon chuckles. "Gallows. That could have multiple meanings there, Ray."

I rub the back of my neck. "Yeah, and I'm really glad it doesn't have the second meaning. Thanks to Savannah and Vinnie's dad."

"That's another thing I don't understand," Falcon says. "Mario Bianchi has all kinds of contacts. There's no reason why his son-in-law had to go to prison."

"Except that he took out the son of a rival," I say.

"Yeah, but they were trying to ally themselves with that family. In fact, they still are. As I understand it, Vinnie is supposed to marry McAllister's daughter."

I cast my gaze to the cold hospital tiles. "I know. Belinda. He's never going to marry her."

"I don't believe he will either. But I do believe that right now, Vinnie is dangerous. If Bianchi is here and Vinnie isn't, then Vinnie's doing business for Bianchi."

I open my mouth to quarrel with Falcon over the statement, but then I close it.

In reality? He's probably right.

Vinnie's a good man.

In my heart of hearts I believe that.

But I also believe that to take down his grandfather—which he swore to do—he's going to have to look the other way in some areas.

Areas I'm better off not knowing about.

But I already know that whatever he has to do, I will forgive him without question.

Because I love him without question.

I love him for everything that he is—everything that he wants to do. And ridding the world of his grandfather is a noble calling.

To make an omelet, you have to break some eggs.

I swallow. "Falcon? Do you believe Vinnie had anything to do with Brick Latham's death?"

"I wondered," he says. "But no, I don't think so."

"I don't think so either," I say, "and I hate myself for saying this, but I wondered as well."

"You did?"

I swallow. "Yes, it crossed my mind. But Brick was killed when he got to our house. And Vinnie was with me when I texted Brick and told him not to come."

Falcon's eyes light up. "Except..."

"Except what?" I ask.

"It just occurred to me. All we truly know is that Brick was found, his car at our house, dead in your bed, his throat slit. We don't know *how* he got there."

32

VINNIE

Austin furrows his brow. "Tell you *what* about Brick Latham? I hardly knew the man."

I clear my throat. "I may have been gone for the last seventeen years, but I wasn't born yesterday. I've been trying to wrap my head around this whole Brick Latham thing. And there's one thing that I can't get past."

He narrows his eyes at me. "What's that?"

"The fact that you and your wife weren't home Friday evening, and neither was Raven."

"Yes, and I'm grateful for that. Otherwise, who knows what might have happened?"

I shift in my seat. "Tell me," I say, "how long have you been having your daughter watched?"

His gaze never leaves mine, but I notice a slight flutter on his left eyelid.

Yes. I'm on to something.

"Are you going to answer me?" I ask.

"I ought to haul your ass out of my house," he says.

I will my body to not flinch. "But you're not going to, and

we both know that." I stand, lean over the front of his desk. "Look. I've got no beef with you. I'll be honest with you and tell you that I'm in love with your daughter. I'm also going to stay away from her because I know that being in my circle right now does not keep her anywhere close to safe."

Austin nods. "Agreed."

"Is it just Raven?" I ask. "Or are you having all of your children watched?"

Austin clears his throat, riffles his fingers through his graying hair. "Walk a mile in my shoes, and then tell me how to be a father."

I hold up a hand. "You're misunderstanding me. I'm not telling you how to be a father. I wouldn't presume to do anything like that. But I interrogated my grandfather about that attorney getting killed on your property. I was certain he had something to do with it. Whether he was trying to implicate Raven or you or somebody else, I didn't know. But he maintains his innocence, Austin. And though he's about as trustworthy as a fox chasing a chicken, the words he said to me made me think."

"What words were those?" Austin asks.

"Suffice it to say that it made me think of you."

"And why did you do that?" He darts his gaze around the room.

I stare him down, not allowing him to break eye contact. "I think you already know why. And by the way, you scared the hell out of your daughter when you hijacked her Uber app."

"I don't know what you're talking about." He drops his gaze to the desk.

"We can play it that way if you'd like. But I'll uncover

what I need to uncover. And I would hate for you to go to prison for the murder of Brick Latham."

He returns his gaze to mine. "That won't happen."

"Won't it? If you had those kind of contacts, you would have kept your own son out of prison."

He doesn't speak for a moment.

I can almost see the cogs working in his brain as he tries to figure out how to handle this. I'm not his enemy, I think he knows that. Just in case—

"I'm not your enemy, Austin. I'm in love with your daughter, which puts us on the same side here."

"I'm not so sure that's the case," he says, slowly rising. "I'm a law-abiding citizen. Never been in trouble a day in my life."

"Except for those records that were expunged. You caused the death of a vendor when you were a teen."

His eyebrows rise slightly. He's trying to hide his surprise. "I don't know what you're talking about."

"You do." I shrug. "You know exactly what I'm talking about. The records may have been wiped once you turned eighteen, and your slate is clean, but that doesn't mean that those records don't exist somewhere out there."

"Jesus fuck," he says.

"Look, I'm not interested in some stupid thing you did when you were a kid. You paid your dues, and I accept that. But don't stand there and tell me you're a pillar of society when the two of us both know you're not."

He cocks his head at me. "Have you looked in the mirror lately?"

"I look in the mirror every day, Austin. I don't always like what I see. But I made a deal with the devil himself, and I'll see it through. I'll see it through for my sister and for my mother. And for my father, who's currently serving time."

"That's puzzling to me," Austin says. "You speak of my contacts. What of yours? People in your grandfather's circle have gotten away with far more."

"Because my father's right where my grandfather wants him," I say. "Which also makes me wonder..."

"Wonder what?"

"If, for eight years, your son was exactly where *you* wanted him."

This time Austin's jaw drops. "I did everything I could to keep him out of the slammer. But because of his name, the prosecution wanted to make an example out of him. They were going to put him through a trial, and it would have made all the papers."

"Yes, and that would've sullied your good Bellamy name." I sit back down, never letting my eyes break contact with his. "You expect me to believe you don't have friends in the judicial department who could have made this go away?"

"I tried. But a cop was killed. You haven't lived in Texas long, but our judiciary doesn't look kindly on cop killers. Plus, he was killed by my son's gun." He sighs. "Do I believe Falcon did it? Absolutely not. But he took the blame. He pleaded guilty. He took the deal for prison time. He was twenty-two years old at the time—a legal adult. There wasn't anything I could do to stop him."

"You know what's interesting?" I ask. "I think there's a part of you that actually believes that."

He glares at me. "I believe it because it's the truth. You think I wanted to see my son go to prison? What father would want that?"

"I'm not accusing you of anything. I'm just looking at what's before my eyes. And quite frankly? I think you just got away with arranging a murder on your property. Funny how it went away so quickly this time. But eight years ago, it didn't."

"You say you're not my enemy," he says. "That's not how you're talking."

I hold up a hand. "I'm not your enemy, Austin. But I'm looking for the truth. Raven's safety is paramount to me. More important than anything. As important as my mother and sister, and honestly? Maybe even more so. I know I can't be with her. That we can't have a life together, but I will do everything I can to keep her safe."

"Then we have the same goal."

"I believe we do." I rise again, leering over the desk at him. "So here's my question to you. Why Brick Latham? Why was he a threat to Raven?"

He crosses his arms. "I don't owe you any explanations."

"You don't. That's true. But if I'm going to see to Raven's protection, I need to know everything you do."

"Falcon hired her a tank of a bodyguard." He looks me up and down. "I don't think she needs your protection."

"Trust me. She needs my protection."

"Why?" He squints at me. "Unless you know something I don't."

"Only that my grandfather knows how I feel about her. That puts her in a bad place. He'll try to use her as leverage against me. I can't allow that to happen. Somehow I have to convince him that I have no feelings for Raven. Which of course means I have to stay away from her. In the meantime, though, you can't use her like that. You can't send an Uber driver to basically kidnap her and tell her to do something. To keep me occupied."

He doesn't respond.

"I see you're not denying it."

He blinks. "There's nothing to deny."

"So I'll ask you again. Are you having all of your children watched? Or only Raven?"

He draws in a breath and lets it out slowly. I know the gesture. He's trying to figure out how to play this. I'm on to him, and he knows it.

Finally, he speaks. "All of them. Since Falcon got put away."

I stop my jaw from dropping. "You've been having your children watched for the last eight years?"

"Why wouldn't I? I couldn't risk any of them getting into trouble like he did. It all could've been prevented if I had known what was going on."

"And tell me this." I walk to the other side of the desk, squatting down to his eye level. "Did you want Falcon in prison?"

He looks away from me. "Whether I wanted him in prison or not is irrelevant. That's where he had to be. It was the only way I could keep the story contained. I didn't want my son branded as a cop killer. I didn't want every tabloid in the free world descending on this ranch. I know damned well Falcon didn't pull that trigger."

"Do you know who did?"

He frowns. "I have my suspicions."

"I see."

Then he does a double take. "Wait. Do *you* know?"

33

RAVEN

I look up when an older man and a young girl walk in to the waiting area. The man is dressed to the nines in a designer suit. The girl is dressed in a pretty blue party dress, complete with lacy ankle socks and patent-leather shoes.

"Caroline Gallo?" The man asks the volunteer on duty.

"Are you family?"

"Friends."

The volunteer frowns. "Then I'm afraid I can't help you. But that's her son-in-law over there. He may be able to help you." She gestures to where Falcon, Jared, and I are seated.

Falcon's jaw drops.

He rises, walks over to the man. "What the hell do you think *you're* doing here?"

"Oh, Mr. Bellamy." When he smiles, he looks like a snake. "I see you're faring well."

"You need to get the fuck out of here now."

He narrows his venomous gaze at Falcon. "I'll thank you to watch your language in front of my daughter."

"Shut up."

"I'd like to know how your future mother-in-law is doing." He scans the room. "I believe Savannah's grandfather is here?"

I don't like where this is going. I walk toward them. "Hello," I say to the girl. "My name is Raven. What's yours?"

"Belinda."

I stop myself from throwing my hand over my mouth. Oh my God. This must be Declan McAllister and his daughter Belinda. This little girl is Vinnie's intended.

But my God… She's just a little girl. She looks like she's going to an afternoon tea party or something.

"Are you thirsty? We could go get a drink." I look up at the man who must be Declan McAllister. "If it's okay with you, sir."

That will get Belinda out of the way so Falcon can have it out with Declan McAllister. He's the father of Miles McAllister, the man Vinnie's father shot to protect Falcon.

And this little girl? She's his sister.

"Don't go too far, Belinda." Her father turns to me. "In fact, if you could just get her a bottle of water and come right back here, I'd appreciate it."

"Is that okay with you?" I ask Belinda. "We'll just go down the hallway and get a drink and bring it right back here." I nod to Jared. "This is Jared. He'll come with us. He's really nice."

Her eyes widen—Jared has that effect on people—but she nods and lets go of her father's hand quickly.

She seems skittish, so I gesture to her without touching her. "It's this way."

We make it to a soda machine, and of course they don't

have Orange Crush. "Would you like something besides water?" I ask.

She shifts her weight from one foot to the other. "I'm not allowed to drink soda. But water's fine." She stares at me.

"You can ask me about my hair," I say. "It's okay. I had cancer. But I'm okay now."

"I'm sorry. I'm glad you're okay."

"Me too." I slide my credit card into the reader and pay for two bottles of water. I hand one to Belinda. "You ready to go back?"

She unscrews the cap of her water and takes a drink. "Do we have to go back?"

I widen my eyes. "Of course. Your father will wonder what happened to you."

She says nothing.

"Belinda, do you want to go somewhere else?"

"Nowhere. Back to my father is fine." She glances around the area nervously. "I just don't want to miss my piano lesson later."

"You play the piano?"

"Yeah." She smiles, her eyes brightening. "I'm really good, too."

"That's great. Nobody in my family has any musical talent."

"No one in my family does either. Daddy says I'm a prodigy."

I smile at her. "That's just wonderful. I understand why you don't want to miss your lesson. I'm sure your father understands as well."

She looks over her shoulder and then returns her gaze to me. "Can I tell you a secret?"

"Sure." I nod to Jared. "Can you give us some privacy? Just far enough so that you can't hear her?"

"Of course." Jared walks several feet away.

I kneel. "What is it, Belinda?"

She cups her hand over her mouth and whispers into my ear. "I know I look small for my age. I'm actually eleven."

"All girls mature at different rates."

"I know. My nanny tells me that all the time."

"See?"

"That's just it. I don't see." She crosses her arms. "I don't go to school with other girls. My nanny teaches me at home."

"Oh. Do you like that?"

She bites her lip. "I like my nanny a lot. She's nice. Sometimes I wish I had a friend."

My heart breaks for this little girl. In seven short years, she's supposed to marry Vinnie. And of course by then she'll have matured into a woman—probably a beautiful one, with the fine features she possesses along with her thick blond hair and light-blue eyes.

But before me is not a woman. Before me is a little girl. A little girl who just wants a friend.

The thought makes my heart ache.

"Maybe you should talk to your dad. Tell him you want a friend."

She shakes her head. "No. I won't talk to him. Not about anything."

"Belind—"

"Please." She grabs my arm, almost desperately. "Don't take me back. Not yet."

I'm not sure what to say to her. She obviously wants a break from her father, but why? Whatever the reason, it's certainly not my place to facilitate it. I don't want to be arrested for kidnapping.

"Belinda, I can't keep you hidden from your father. It wouldn't be right," I say, gently but firmly.

Her eyes well up with tears.

A pang of guilt seizes me.

"I know. I just... I just don't want to go back there yet." She chokes on her words. Her eyes are pleading, her small hand clutching the bottle of water so tight it looks like it might burst.

"All right," I say reluctantly. "We can stay here a little longer."

We sit silently on a bench near the soda machine. I watch as she picks at a loose thread on her dress, her blue eyes vacant and far away. The drone of conversations is muffled around us.

"Can I tell you another secret?" Belinda asks, her voice barely more than a whisper.

"Of course."

She gulps. "I'm scared. I'm scared of my father."

My heart clenches. Her blue eyes are filled with fear and a sorrow that no child should have to bear. She looks down and plays with the hem of her dress.

"Why?" I ask, though deep down I fear I know the answer.

"He gets angry. He screams, and..."

I gently place my hand over hers, trying to offer some semblance of comfort. Meanwhile inside I'm a storm of anger and sadness.

"I'm sorry to hear that, Belinda," I say. "But he doesn't hurt you, does he?"

She swallows.

"I can't tell," she finally says.

A sickening knot forms in my stomach. My mind whirls with thoughts and emotions, struggling to process the implications of her words.

"I see." I can barely control the tremor in my voice. "Belinda, if anything bad happens, you should tell someone about it. Someone you trust."

She looks at me, her eyes filled with innocent confusion. "I have. My nanny. She's trying."

I squeeze her hand. "I'm sure she's trying her best."

"You're kind," Belinda says. "I think I can trust *you*, Raven."

Her words strike me, and I swallow the lump in my throat. "Belinda, I promise to do everything in my power to help you. But in the meantime, we need to go back, okay?"

She looks down, kicking at the floor for a moment. "I guess so," she finally says quietly.

We return to the waiting area to find Declan McAllister pacing.

"You were gone a long time just getting a drink," he says.

"She just wanted to talk a little bit," I tell him. "I think she's lonely."

"She's just fine. She has me." He takes the girl's hand. "You should mind your own business," he says under his breath.

But I heard him.

And beside me, Falcon is seething.

34

VINNIE

"Wait. Do *you* know?"

"You feel like making a deal, Austin?"

"Am I dealing with the grandson of Mario Bianchi? Or with the man who loves my daughter?"

"The two are one and the same," I tell him. "We can have this talk if you like, but I need your guarantee that it doesn't leave this room. That there's no surveillance system recording us."

He frowns. "I can't guarantee that."

I rise from my squatting position and head toward the office door. "Then I suppose we're done here."

"No. I don't want to be done." He rises. "Come with me."

We leave his office, and together we walk out the front door.

"I need to check with my driver and my bodyguard," I say.

"They're in the car?"

"Yes. The air conditioning is on. They're fine."

"They're not dogs, Vinnie. They're people. They can wait in the house if you like."

I shrug. "This is what they're used to. Trust me that the car is comfortable. But thank you for the offer."

He leads me to a small bench off the porch of the house. "We can speak freely here." He pulls out his phone. "See? Not recording anything."

"All right," I say. I take a deep breath in before continuing. "Here's the deal. I want to know who Brick Latham was. And why he's no longer alive."

He gazes out onto his land. "I didn't find out about his connections until after Raven already met with him. When I found out that she had a date with him—"

"And you found that out because you're having her watched, correct?"

He snaps his head back at me, his eyes fiery. "I'm not going to keep defending myself for that. My wife doesn't know about it, and I'd like to keep it that way. But after what went down eight years ago..."

"Right." I'm still not sure I believe him about all of that. I think he had another reason for wanting Falcon in prison, but I'm just not sure what it is. "You don't need to go through all of that again. I get it."

"Right. So this Latham, he spent a lot of time with Raven that day here at the house. They worked on the setup for her nonprofit that she wants to start."

"Right. I know all about that. A worthy endeavor."

"Yeah, it is. A great idea for her. Because he spent so much time here, I looked into it."

"Isn't he with a firm that you do business with?"

"He is. Turns out he's a bit...unethical, according to his partners. They've been trying to figure out a way to oust him for years."

"Okay." I press my lips together. "That doesn't explain why you got involved."

"No, it doesn't. I did some research. Probably similar to the research you did when you found out about my infractions when I was a minor."

Interesting. So Austin Bellamy is no stranger to the dark web. That's not necessarily a bad thing.

"What did you find out?"

"He came into some money about five years ago. It was laundered through a dry cleaner in Austin."

I nod slowly. "So I can understand that you wouldn't want your daughter dating a money launderer. But I'm still not sure why—"

"I'm not finished," he says. "He's used the money to pay people off. No less than eight women have accused him of rape."

Chills run through me.

"So you can see my dilemma," he says.

"Yes, I do."

"I don't go around ordering the deaths of people," he says. "This is only the second time I've ever done it."

"Who did you have offed the first time?"

"I don't think that's any of your business, Mr. Gallo."

He's right. It's probably not. Unless it was Diego Vega, but I'm still pretty sure Austin doesn't know anything about that.

"I couldn't let my daughter get into that."

"So you arranged to have her out of the house—with me—and your wife and you were also out of the house."

"That's correct. Alibis all around."

"Then why didn't you go into Raven's room as soon as you got home? It would've made your alibis cleaner."

"For the same reason you would've done the same thing. My wife had to be the one to find him. It couldn't be me."

"And you knew she would check on Raven in the morning."

"Exactly."

I'm not sure whether to have respect for the man or contempt. Why would he put his wife through finding a dead body in his daughter's bed when he could have done all of this miles away from here?

That's pretty cold.

But Austin Bellamy had his reasons, I'm sure. It was in his best interest to have it done at his house. In a way, it made him look even more innocent.

"All right. You should know, though, that my grandfather's on to you."

He scoffs. "I'm not afraid of Mario Bianchi."

"You should be," I tell him. "I believe you're a good man. I believe you do bad things sometimes to protect those you love. I get that. But Mario Bianchi? He's *not* a good man. Whatever good he had inside him was erased long ago. He knows what happened, and if he wanted to, he could expose you."

He crosses his arms. "Then you and I need to make sure that doesn't happen."

"You're right. We do." I lean in, lowering my voice. "I plan to take him down, but my plan was always to do that in my own time. I want to protect my mother, my sister, myself. And now Raven. I didn't know I was going to have to protect you and your wife too."

He shakes his head. "I can protect my wife just fine. I've done it for the last thirty years."

"I don't think my grandfather's any threat to you." I look into his eyes. "But just be aware that he knows. If the day comes when he needs to use it as leverage or needs a favor from you, he won't hesitate."

"I can't imagine why your grandfather would ever need anything from me."

"You'd be surprised."

"That may or may not be, but for now, Vinnie, we had a deal." He grits his teeth. "Tell me who shot that cop, because I know it wasn't my son."

I don't know Austin Bellamy well yet, but I do know that he will protect his children.

As long as it serves his own interests.

I believe he could have kept Falcon out of prison, which is why I'm not going to level with him now.

I open my mouth to say as much when my phone buzzes.

It's Raven.

"I'm so sorry, I have to take this."

I stand and walk out of earshot from Austin.

"Raven?" I say into the phone.

"Vinnie, I know you don't want to hear from me, but I'm afraid you're going to have to."

"Is my mother okay?"

"Yes, she's fine. Savannah's in with her. And your grandfather is still here. But your mother has some other visitors."

"Oh?"

"Yeah. Declan McAllister, and his daughter."

Shit. "Raven, you know—"

"That's not what this is about, Vinnie. I know you're not going to marry her. Or maybe you will someday. Who knows?

My concern isn't about that. It's for the little girl. I think her father is... He's hurting her, Vinnie."

Fuck. Belinda must be getting desperate if she told Raven—a stranger—what's going on. "What makes you think that?"

"I offered to take her to get a drink while her father talked to your grandfather and went to see your mother."

"I don't want that degenerate anywhere near my mother."

"Yeah, I can understand that. Anyway, she was so timid, and frankly I was surprised he let her go with Jared and me. But he did, and she didn't want to go back to him. She wanted to hang out with me for a little while. She didn't talk much at first, just told me how much she likes playing the piano."

I sigh. "I know about this, Raven. I'm trying to figure out how to deal with it."

"You know?"

"Yes. I had lunch with McAllister and his daughter a couple days ago. She slipped me a note asking for help. And then I talked to the nanny later and she told me about her father hurting her."

"What are you doing about it?"

"I haven't been able to do anything about it. I'm supposed to be in Colombia right now. And once my mother's out of danger, I know my grandfather's going to want me back on that plane."

"You can't get on the plane, Vinnie."

"Raven, I'm not going to have a choice."

"This is the woman you're supposed to marry." Her voice is pleading. "You can't just let her stay in harm's way."

"First of all, Raven, she's not a woman. She's a little girl. And I'm not going to marry her. I hate this as much as you do. But there's one thing I know about this family that I've been so fortunate enough to be born into," I say sarcastically. "He may be hurting her, but he'll make sure she stays a virgin. That's part of the deal."

"Great, so he's not fucking her. There are a lot of other things he could be doing to her."

I pause a moment. "I know that. Did you see any bruises on her?"

"No, I didn't."

"What was she dressed in?"

"Some kind of party dress. The girl is eleven, but I swear he dresses her to look like she's six."

"Yeah, I know." I run my hands through my hair. "It's beyond disturbing. I wish we could help her. I really do. The fact that he's hurting her makes me ache inside. But her life isn't in danger, Raven. Her virginity isn't in danger."

"I can't even believe you're saying these things, Vinnie." She starts crying. "How did I ever think I loved you?"

Those words cut into my heart like a knife.

But I can use them to my advantage. For Raven's protection, she needs to stay away from me. And if she hates me? That will make it all the easier.

The idea of making her hate me breaks my heart. I love her so much. I know she loves me too. But if I let her see a side of me that she doesn't like...

Perhaps she'll at least stay away.

"Raven," I say, "it's not my problem."

I hear her gasp, and then she ends the call abruptly.

I feel like a fucking heel. I ache for that little girl as much as she does. And I will find a way to help her, but I think it's better if Raven thinks I won't.

She's seeing that I may not be the man she thinks I am.

And although she's wrong, letting her think that will work in my favor. At least for now.

I shove my phone in my pocket and go back to Austin.

"Is your mother okay?" he asks me.

Of course. He thought the call was about my mother. He has no idea it was his own daughter on the other end of the line.

"She's not good," I lie. "I should be getting back to her."

"We have an understanding then?"

"Yes. No one will hear anything from me about Brick Latham." The world is better off without one more rapist and money launderer. I'm just grateful that Raven didn't end up in his clutches.

"Good. And you have something to tell me?"

I pause a moment.

Cobra.

I haven't brought up the name on purpose. Now that I know that Bellamy was behind Latham's demise, I know something else as well. He knows more than he's letting on about what happened years ago.

And Diego Vega.

Only my father, my grandfather, and Vega knew about that nickname for me, and it's not something Bellamy would have found on the dark web.

Which means...

"Later," I say. "My mother takes precedence."

35

RAVEN

I walk back to the waiting area and sit next to Falcon.

"What did he say?" he asks me.

"He... He says he knows what's going on. But there's nothing he can do about it." I gulp. "He says it's not his problem."

Falcon's jaw drops.

"I know. I can't believe it either. Is he not the man I thought he was?" I bury my face in my hands.

Falcon tilts his head, and I wait for him to speak. When he doesn't—

"Are you going to answer me?"

He wraps his arm around my shoulders. "There's a lot we don't know about him. He was gone for seventeen years. We don't know what he did over there, other than what he told Savannah."

"He mentioned that he spent some time in a Buddhist temple. Where he ate nothing but rice and lentils."

"And that's supposed to make him an upstanding human being?"

"I don't know. He doesn't talk about it much." I shrug. "But seventeen years. That's a long time."

"More than twice the time I spent behind bars," Falcon says. "I don't know much about him, Raven. Only that Savannah loves him, which is really all I need to know. But without going into too much detail, the reason he left was because his grandfather did something really horrific to him."

I wipe a tear from my cheek. "What?"

"I can't say anything more than that. He told Savannah, and he probably didn't want her to tell me, but she did."

"You and Savannah are going to be married. You shouldn't have any secrets."

"We don't. Not now, anyway."

I nod. He's talking about what happened eight years ago. Because my father was going to excavate on that part of the property, and Falcon needed Vinnie's help, he had to level with Savannah and Vinnie. And me? I just happened to be in the right place at the right time to overhear them.

I run my hand over my peach-fuzz head. "I just don't know. I thought he would help that little girl."

"Vinnie's not a stupid man. If he says he can't help her, he has a reason."

"I'm beginning to rethink everything," I say. "I love him more than I love my next breath of air, but maybe… Maybe sometimes you have to follow your head instead of your heart."

Falcon nods. "Unfortunately, sometimes you do. I'll be the first person to give you the advice to follow your heart, Ray. Especially after what you've been through. But I also value your life. You fought hard to have one. I don't want to see you put in jeopardy."

"Yeah. You're right." I rise and signal to Jared. "I think I want to go home, Falcon. I don't think I'm needed here. Would you keep me advised of Caroline's situation?"

"Yeah, of course."

We both jerk as Mario Bianchi, Declan McAllister, and Belinda walk by, but we regain our composure quickly.

I smile at Belinda and wave.

She looks away from me.

Once they're back out of earshot, I turn to my brother. "God, Falcon. She went to Vinnie for help. She came to *me* for help. And I had known her for all of fifteen seconds when she did. I can't just turn away from her."

Falcon takes a deep breath in. "I don't think you have a choice."

"I can call social services, tell them what I think is going on."

"It wouldn't do any good, and you know it. Declan McAllister's way more powerful than anyone in social services. Belinda is probably trained like a seal in exactly what to say. Most likely they've been through it before."

I sigh. My brother is no doubt right. The nanny knows and has been trying to help her for ages, I'm sure. Social services would have been her first call.

But it just pains me to think of what may be happening to that little girl.

Why does he dress her like that? She's eleven. Not seven.

"Are you ready, Raven?" Jared asks.

"Yeah. Let's go home."

I DON'T STOP at my parents' house on the way home. Instead, I instruct Jared to take me to my own home. It's time I move in and get on with my life. I'm perfectly safe here with the state-of-the-art security and, of course, Jared.

Once I'm home, I tell Jared I'm going to my room to do some work on my foundation.

Brick got me started, but now it's time for me to use my name and make some phone calls.

I need funding, and I want to begin with a big gala.

I'll foot the bill myself from my own trust fund.

It's time to let Vinnie go.

And concentrate on my own life, what's important to me.

He has his job to do.

And so do I.

36

VINNIE

I get back to the hospital, and my grandfather and Declan McAllister are no longer there. Falcon is sitting in the waiting area.

"Just you?"

He looks up at me, his gaze wary. His tone is artificially even as he speaks to me. "Savannah's in with your mother. She's coming in and out of consciousness. I'm sure she'll be happy to see you."

I walk back to my mother's room.

Savannah is sitting next to the bed, holding onto my mother's frail hand. "Hey, Vinnie," she says.

"Hey." I squeeze her shoulder. "Why don't you go? I'll sit with her for a while. I'm sorry I was gone for so long."

"She'll be happy to see you." She lets out a light laugh. "She was even pretty happy to see me."

"She loves you, Sav. You know that."

"I know. I just have to accept the fact that women aren't as valuable as men in her world."

I lean in and lower my voice. "Her world won't be around for much longer if I have anything to say about it."

She lets go of Mom's hand and rises. "I'll go sit with Falcon for a while in the waiting area. Let me know if she wakes up or if you need me for anything."

"Will do." I take the chair where Savannah was sitting. "And Sav?"

She turns in the doorway. "Yeah?"

I sigh. "Hold on to Falcon. He's a good guy."

She smiles. "Don't I know it." She leaves the ICU unit.

I redirect my attention to my mother, grabbing her hand. "I'm here, Mom."

Her eyelids flutter. "Vinnie?" she rasps out.

I squeeze her hand. "Yeah, I'm here."

She winces. "I have to...tell you something."

"Okay."

"You need to know." She closes her eyes. "You were always my favorite. Even after how you came into the world."

I smile. "It was a tough labor. I know."

"No. I mean..." Her voice cracks. "Your grandfather..."

"Yes, I know he was here."

"Your father..."

"I'm working with our attorneys to get him a furlough to come see you."

"Yes. But no. I mean. Your father..."

I wrinkle my forehead. What is she trying to say? "Yes, Mom? What is it?"

"He... Your father is..." She shifts in her bed. The heart monitor accelerates.

"Easy." I put her hand down, patting it lightly. "You'll tell me later."

"No..." She opens her eyes, grimacing. "Must tell you..."

The alarms on the machines start blaring.

"Oh my God, Mom!" My pulse races as fear courses through me.

Her eyes close.

The room floods with nurses.

"Sir, you're going to have to leave," one of them says to me.

"What? What's wrong?"

Just as I ask this, a doctor rushes in, his face grim.

"No, I need to stay. She was trying to tell me something about my dad!" I yell over the tumultuous drone of the machines.

The doctor pushes past the nurses, immediately attending to my mom. He moves quickly. "Code blue!"

"Sir, you have to leave!" The same nurse's voice cuts through the cacophony again, hands guiding me towards the door.

"No! You don't understand—"

But before I can finish my plea, I find myself in the hallway outside the room. The door slams shut behind me, cutting off any protest.

I collapse against the cold hospital wall, staring at the closed door. My mind swims with questions left unanswered as the reality sinks in.

What was my mother trying to tell me?

And what is happening to her now?

I stand in the doorway of her room.

"She may have thrown a clot," someone says. "Get a heparin drip started. We've got to get her pulse ox up or we're going to lose her."

My heart drops as I hear the words. A cold shiver slinks

down my spine. I feel like I'm spinning, crashing into a world of fear and uncertainty. An invisible weight presses down on my chest, making it hard to breathe.

My mother, my strength, my anchor throughout my life might be taken from me tonight. And that secret she was about to share remains a secret. The urgency in her voice still rings in my ears as I pound my fists against the wall.

Through the small window on the door, I see them working ceaselessly on Mom. But their quick movements look like they're fading, becoming slower. The doctor's face is a harrowing mask of grim determination and worry.

Then the dreadful words.

"We're losing her."

The painful beep of the flatline haunts the air around me.

"No!" I find myself screaming, "Fight, Mom! Fight!" I rush through the door before a strong hand grabs me by my shoulder, pulling me back. It's another doctor, someone I haven't seen before.

"Son," he says in a deep, sorrowful voice, "we're doing everything we can."

I try to shake him off in an attempt to rush into the room, but his grip is iron. He's used to family members trying to get inside. I sink to the floor, my legs unable to support me anymore.

"I need... She was..." I gulp. "She was saying something about my dad."

I am helpless. Powerless. Just an observer as the doctors and nurses scramble around desperately trying to revive my mother.

The seconds turn into minutes, each ticking away with excruciating slowness.

And then...
"I'm so sorry. We did everything we could."

37

RAVEN

A *week later...*

I wish I could stand next to Vinnie at the funeral. I wish he wanted me there.

I wish everything were different.

I remember eating dinner with Caroline Gallo and her son. How lovely she was. Beautiful. Vinnie looks so much like her. Same hair, same olive skin.

Next to Vinnie stands his father, Vincent Gallo Senior. He was able to get furlough to attend his wife's funeral.

Falcon stands next to Savannah, of course, as her fiancé.

The minister drones on and on about Caroline. Mario Bianchi of course stands there too. His only child, now dead.

I try to listen.

Truly, I do.

Jared sits beside me in the last pew of the grand, old-world Catholic cathedral of Austin. Muted colors from the stained-glass windows scatter across the sanctuary, and the air is thick with the scent of incense. Dark fabrics drape over the pews and altar, and black candles flicker throughout the church. Large, ornate floral arrangements in white and red roses—which, combined with the green of their stems, make up the colors of the Italian flag—are strewn about the space.

I can't help admiring the polished mahogany coffin in the center of the church, which is flanked by towering candle stands with a simple white rose bouquet resting on top.

"They certainly spared no expense," I whisper to Jared.

His face is grave. "They probably do a lot of funerals in their line of work."

I'm not sure how to respond to that. So I don't.

Jared's presence has become tolerable. More than tolerable, to be honest. I've grown to consider him a friend. I have someone to talk to when I need it, and he's been helping me with my foundation, which is great.

All the paperwork has been filed, and the gala is planned for about a month from now.

One of the best hotels in Austin.

Celebrities, politicians, all the elites have been invited.

I expect it will be a splash.

I tried to speak to Vinnie before the service, but he walked away when he saw me.

I'll let him have his grief. He deserves that much.

And maybe… Just maybe it's time to let go.

I have my whole life ahead of me. A life I wasn't sure I'd get to have.

I can't waste it on someone who doesn't want me.

After the service, Jared and I walk out of the church, avoiding the receiving line. I don't want to look at Vinnie. I'm only here because my brother is engaged to the daughter of the deceased.

As we reach the parking lot, I hear a buzz from my purse.

I reach in, but it's not my normal phone that buzzed.

It's the burner.

I've been carrying it around with me just in case the Uber driver—or whoever is on the other end—needs to get in touch with me.

Jared's eyebrows rise when I pull it out. "What did they say?"

I pull up the text. Three simple words send my heart into violent tremors.

You're in danger.

38

VINNIE

Savannah and I get through the funeral and the burial, though I'm not sure how.

Later, when I'm driving my father back to prison where he will surrender himself, I ask him something.

"Mom was trying to tell me something about you, Dad. Do you know what it was?"

He raises his eyebrows. "No, I have no idea."

"She wasn't making any sense." I scratch my chin. "First she said something about Grandfather. Then about you. She said she had to tell me, and then the alarms started going off on her machines."

"And we lost her..." he says quietly.

"Yes. So you can understand my issue. She was trying to tell me something, and I got the feeling that it was important. Something that she'd kept from me for far too long."

He draws in a long breath. "I wish I knew, son. But I don't. If it was about your grandfather, I probably wouldn't know anyway. And if it was about me?" He shrugs. "You know everything about me, Vinnie. You know that my marriage to your mother was arranged, that my father was your grandfather's consigliore. That I was a golden boy, considered to be the best match for your mother. I'm afraid I disappointed your grandfather greatly on that."

"But you loved Mom."

"We grew to love each other, yes. And now? I can't think of anyone from my past I'd rather spend my life with. It's just as well that I'll be incarcerated for the rest of it, because I can't imagine life without your mother."

"No, Dad. You can't think that way. I'm going to get you out of there. When I take over—"

"No, Vinnie. I killed a man in cold blood."

"It was hardly cold blood. You were defending Falcon." I inhale deeply, steeling myself to ask the one question I'm not supposed to ask. "Is he the first man you killed?"

My father doesn't answer.

Which is, of course, the answer.

"You killed Miles McAllister to save Falcon because you knew Savannah loved him. It wasn't in self-defense, but it was defense of another."

He rubs at the bridge of his nose. "None of that matters anymore. Let me stay in prison, son. I'm safe there. No one dares lay a hand on me because they know who my father-in-law is."

Indeed, my father does not have a scratch on him. For which I'm eternally grateful.

"But I can get you out."

He shakes his head. "I don't *want* to get out. I want to pay for my crimes. And some of them I *am* sorry for." He frowns. "But I'm not sorry for killing Miles McAllister. God only knows what he would've done to Savannah. Thank God she was able to protect herself from him. As her father, I should have been the one to do that."

"You did, Dad. You let her go to college, and then you let her work as a parole officer instead of marrying that derelict."

He swallows, looking down. "But in the end, I couldn't save her. She was going to have to marry him."

"Don't forget that she went to him of her own accord. She thought she was doing it to save Falcon from another prison sentence."

"Yes, Falcon's prison sentence." He frowns, scratching his temple. "Something about that doesn't make sense to me."

"It doesn't make sense to me either. Austin Bellamy is keeping something from me."

"Texas ranching is a funny business sometimes," Dad says. "Ranchers often have their own sordid secrets."

"You and Mom haven't lived in Texas that long."

"No, but my guess is that Austin Bellamy has his own secrets, and unfortunately his son had to pay for one of them."

"What do you know?"

"Vinnie, if I had information that could help you, you know I would tell you. It's only a hunch."

"Are you sure? Because someone had to go down for the killing of that young cop."

"Yes. But the Bellamy family could have found someone else to sacrifice other than one of their own sons."

My father's right, of course. The Bellamy Ranch employs hundreds. Anyone could have been out that night. Anyone could have gotten hold of Falcon's gun.

I have a feeling that the Bellamy ranch shrouds more secrets than perhaps even Austin Bellamy himself knows.

"I believe Falcon is a good man," I say.

"I do as well. Otherwise I wouldn't have saved his ass."

"What about his brothers?"

He shrugs. "I wasn't able to find out too much about them before I had to go to prison. The older one, Hawk, seems good. But I sense that the younger one is a bit of a loose cannon."

My father has no idea.

"I'll look into all of them," I say. "I'll make sure Savannah is safe."

He gives a weak smile. "I know you will, Vinnie."

"I should've been here, Dad." I run my hands through my hair, sighing. "If I had been, Mikey would still be alive."

"I'll never stop mourning your brother," he says. "Just as I'll never stop mourning your mother." He looks at me, a small glimmer of light in his eyes. "But I have you, and I have Savannah. I trust Falcon to keep Savannah safe. And you know what I need you to do."

"I'll do it, Dad. You have my word."

I drop him off at the prison, and when I get back to my mother's home—now *my* home—my grandfather is waiting for me at the front door.

"I have nothing to say to you." I brush past him, opening the door.

"Check your email," he says. "You're back on that flight to Colombia. Leaving tonight."

"Send someone else." I take a step inside the house.

"Nope. I'm sending you." He grabs my arm. "You want to be my second-in-command? That's who I need on this mission. You'd be there now if your mother hadn't had that heart attack."

I grit my teeth. "Don't even talk about my mother."

He frowns, laying a hand over his heart. "You think this isn't killing me? She was my child."

"Yes. Your only child."

His lips twitch.

And I cock my head.

"My mother was trying to tell me something before she died. Something about you. Something about my father."

He raises an eyebrow. "You mean you haven't guessed?"

I whip my arm out of his grasp. "Stop playing games with me, old man. If there's something I need to know about my father, you need to tell me."

"All you need to know about Vincent Gallo Senior is that he's a weakling." Grandfather scowls.

"Weak men don't kill a man to save their daughter from marriage to a degenerate."

He says nothing.

"So don't ever tell me my father's a weak man again."

"To the contrary," he says, "your father is the strongest man I know."

"But you just said—"

I gulp as the truth hits me.

Hard.

Like a fucking boulder.

Oh my God.

What my mother was trying to tell me...

What my grandfather just said...

A sharp, prickling sensation creeps across my skin, as if every nerve is freezing in place, leaving me numb and rigid.

There's a reason I look so much like my mother, so much like my grandfather. How adamant he was about wishing he'd never sold my mother off to my father. How resolute he was when he said *his* blood flows through my veins.

And my father doesn't know. *He doesn't know.*

And all mafia brides are supposed to be virgins...

Nausea grips me, but I resist the urge to double over and retch.

"You fucking bastard," I grit out.

A wicked grin crawls across his wrinkled face. "Now, Vincent," he sneers. "Is that any way to speak to your *father?*"

VINNIE AND RAVEN'S story continues in *Victorious Vice!*

EXCERPT FROM ENTICING YOU

PREVIOUSLY PUBLISHED ON KINDLE VELLA AS HOW TO MARRY A BILLIONAIRE, COMING SOON TO PRINT FOR THE FIRST TIME!

Play the ultimate game of love and money! Four powerful billionaires, bound by their Montana roots and one devastating secret, escape to a secluded tropical island to find love. Eight stunning women, harboring their own secrets, compete for the men's affections. *The Bachelor* meets *Yellowstone* in this high-stakes, pulse-pounding story. Heat sizzles among the men and women, but beneath the sun-drenched surface, mysteries simmer, ready to explode...

1
A Little Mermaid in a Big Pond

Ariel

My heart thumps so hard I can see it against the teal satin of my strapless dress.

Excerpt from Enticing a BillionaireI don't belong here.

This dress isn't me.

These slinky silver sandals with spiky heels aren't me.

This whole place...so not me.

Yet here I am, about to meet four billionaires who are on this island to find wives.

The other women are way more beautiful and worldly than I am. Evangeline found me at an old-fashioned drive-in diner serving food on roller skates in my small hometown in Alabama. I delivered a loaded burger, curly fries, and diet soda—cue eye roll—to her car, and when she saw me, she removed her designer sunglasses and burned me with her dark eyes.

"You married?" she asked.

"Hell, no. If I had a husband, I wouldn't be working this shitty job."

"Oh?"

"Of course not. Any boy I marry has to be rich."

She cocked her head, raked her gaze down my body, and then back up again. "You're perfect."

"Perfect for what?"

"You want to marry a rich boy? How about a rich man? How about a billionaire?"

I nearly dropped the tray before I got it latched to her car.

"I asked if you want to marry a billionaire," she said. "Aren't you going to say anything?"

I narrowed my eyes at the classy woman who clearly wasn't from around here. "Yeah. You can use the app on your phone to pay, or we take credit, debit, or cash."

"I guess you're not serious about wanting to marry that rich boy." She let out a laugh that sounded just like she looked—judgy and rich.

"Oh, I'm serious about marrying money. I just wasn't born yesterday."

I skated away, but Evangeline—I didn't know her name

yet—got out of her car, followed me into the diner, and made me an offer I'd have been an idiot to refuse.

Two days later, I arrived here—on Billionaire Island, as we call it.

That was two weeks ago. Since then, I've learned all about Evangeline and the whirlwind adventure that sounded way too good to be true when I had skates on my feet and red Alabama dust in my hair. This isn't a reality show. No cameras, no videos. Billionaire Island is a life-changing opportunity for the right women. Too bad I won't be one of the "right" ones. But that didn't stop me from accepting the all-expenses paid trip, the free wardrobe, and the high-class makeover.

Now I'm wearing clothes that aren't mine, my hair is a color that looks way more natural on me than what I got from Mama, and I'm lined up with a dozen other girls like a wannabe in the Miss Alabama pageant. Today's the day. The billionaires have arrived.

Evangeline briefed us on the men we're here to meet.

River Barrett, a rancher.

Brett Dawson, an entrepreneur.

Sebastian Tate, a rock star.

Alex Maxwell, a bestselling author.

Sebastian Tate is the only one I'd heard of before coming here. I don't run in billionaire circles, obviously, and though I'm more of a country music fan, everyone knows who he is. I don't know anything about ranching or business, and I can't recall the last time I've read anything other than Cosmopolitan. We've been briefed on all of them, though—their hobbies, their likes, their dislikes, what they're looking for in a woman, pretty much everything except their freaking dick sizes, which frankly would be nice to know.

They're all rich and gorgeous, so why do they want to meet women this way? Of course, I got a free vacation and an amazing designer wardrobe out of it so I'm not complaining.

No way will I snag one of them, though. Not with Juniper Loring and Emily Kensington standing on either side of me. June is a lingerie model from Manhattan, and Emily is a fashion designer from London. We've also got an attorney, a hair stylist, an heiress—why she needs to marry a billionaire is beyond me—a dermatologist, and a physicist.

Yes, a physicist. Seriously.

We're a virtual who's who of smart and gorgeous women with impressive resumés.

Until you get to me, that is.

Ariel Tanner, a roller waitress who left school at sixteen and whose mother named her after a cartoon character.

Evangeline added auburn highlights to my light brown hair, and this skin-tight mini-dress is a rich, exotic teal—just like the waters outside the palatial mansion where we've been staying. Add a sequined tail, and I'll be true to my name.

The eight of us—yes, there are eight women for only four men—stand in a row outside the back of the mansion, facing the large courtyard.

"Ladies"—Evangeline raises her hands—"the gentlemen will be here shortly! Let's prepare to give them a welcome!"

I strike the pose I've been practicing thanks to Evangeline's constant corrections—shoulders back, hips forward, right foot out, seductive smile. For some of the girls, smiling means showing a little bit of teeth. For me it means lips only, curved slightly upward.

"Your lips are so hot even I want to kiss you," Evangeline told me. "Use them to your advantage."

All eight of us are on display—a smorgasbord of tits and ass. At least I can compete with the others in that department.

But what billionaire is going to want just tits and ass when he can have tits, ass, beauty, and brains?

"For the love of God," Emily says under her breath. "Let's get on with it already."

I stifle a chuckle. Of all the women here, Emily is the one I like the most. She's always got something to say. We have that in common.

I don't dare reply, though I'm thinking the same thing. When Evangeline told us to get into position, I figured the men would be here in a minute or two. My nerves are doing a line dance under my skin.

Evangeline, who looks naturally goth with her dark hair and eyes, creamy fair skin, and lithe frame, walks toward us, looking us over. We're arranged by height, the shortest of us on each end, and the tallest in the middle.

"Emily, try not to look like you'd rather be anywhere but here," Evangeline chides, "and Ariel, you're slouching."

I breathe in and pull my shoulders back.

"Better. Remember, you're meeting a potential husband, not waiting for a hayride." She steps away from me. "June, perfect as always."

Perfect as always. Of course she's perfect. She's a professional model. A professional lingerie model, with honey blond hair, blue eyes, and perfect proportions. She's not the most beautiful, though. That title goes to Dr. Ginger Swanson, the dermatologist, whose oval face, strawberries-and-cream blush, long dark hair, green eyes, and gorgeous curves scream 1940s pinup girl.

Me? I'm Ariel, the hayseed mermaid.

"Misty"—Evangeline pulls a tissue out of her black leather and chrome studded evening bag—"you've got lipstick on your teeth."

Misty Holmes—she's the heiress; her father is Barker Holmes of the Holmes hotel empire—bares her teeth while Evangeline wipes away the red smudges and then continues down our line, pointing out deficiencies, until she reaches for her phone.

"They're coming!" She smiles. "You know what to do."

Yes.

Shoulders back.

Hips forward.

Right foot slightly in front of left.

Seductive smile, no teeth.

Soft music from a real string quartet playing on the large terrace wafts through the air. The light tropical breeze brings with it the aroma of roast pork, the centerpiece of the spread already laid out for us to nosh on later as we mingle with the men.

I focus my gaze on the vibrant greenery, bright exotic flowers, and tall palm trees swaying in the warm, gentle breeze, and in the distance, the private white sand beach and sparkling blue ocean.

Still, my breath catches and excitement races through me. I've come to paradise to meet four billionaires. Not one of them will give me a glance, of course, but at least I've made some awesome memories, eaten some delicious food, even made a friend—sort of—in Emily. Not bad for a roller waitress from Alabama.

The French doors behind us click open.

Shoulders back.

Hips forward.

Right leg extended slightly.

Damn. Why can't I open my mouth? I need to suck in a breath.

Because though I've seen photos and videos, these men are even more spectacular in person.

River Barrett, the rancher, holds a black cowboy hat in muscular hands. His hair is dark and wavy, his eyes intense and brown, and the way his dark blue jeans hug his thighs draws my gaze, making me want to squirm, until I have to force myself to look at the next man.

Brett Dawson is an entrepreneur who devised some software something or other that I guess revolutionized remote business. Whatever. What I care about is his sun-bleached blond hair that reminds me of a California surfer boy. His navy suit brings out his blue eyes that are the color of the clearest summer day back home. He's the only one who wears a tie, and he loosens it as he gazes at us one by one.

Alex Maxwell doesn't look like a bestselling author, although I guess I've never met a real author before. He's got brown hair, hazel eyes, and he's wearing a black blazer, black pants, and a white shirt, but it's the no tie that gets me. I love a man in a suit with his shirt open and no tie. A flutter ripples through my belly.

Sebastian Tate, the rock star, wears faded jeans and a black shirt. His long brown hair is tied back in a low ponytail, and his amber eyes are long lashed and smoldering. My heart pounds. This guy is famous. Really freaking famous, and he's here—he and his three equally gorgeous friends.

I close my eyes without meaning to and inhale a deep breath. I need to get a grip. Evangeline provided our bios to the men, so there won't be any formal introductions. Still, my nerves are skittering. I'm sure all four of them will flock to Juniper or Ginger, but intense heat rakes along my body.

Maybe.

Just maybe one of them will talk to me... Give me more than just a toe-curling look...

I prepare to open my eyes when a deep voice sings into my soul.

"Would you like to join me for a drink, Ariel?

2
Blunt Emily

Emily

"What the hell?" Misty Holmes, the hotel heiress, says to me, glancing toward Ariel. "He's going for *her*?"

"Why wouldn't he?" I ask. "She's lovely, really. Different, yes, but lovely."

Misty scoffs, tossing her light blond hair. "Evangeline was desperate. She had another woman lined up, but she dropped out at the last minute. Is this the first pretty girl she could find? You and I both know she's a poor man's substitute."

"That's rubbish." I glance around. "You're just jealous,

though for the life of me I don't understand why. You don't need to marry for money, so why are you even here?"

"Hey, Evangeline came to *me*. I didn't go to her."

"You're serious?" I raise my eyebrows.

"Of course I'm serious. Didn't she come to you, as well?"

I smooth my hair against the light salt-scented breeze. "Yes, she did. I just assumed—"

"You just assumed because I'm nearly as rich as these men that she wouldn't bother with someone like me."

"It's not that. Not exactly, anyway. We're all well off, it seems."

"Not your little hillbilly friend."

Misty's not wrong, though she's being a witch. Ariel's a good kid. She's the youngest of all of us, at a mere twenty-two years old. Most of the others are in their mid-twenties. The men are all the same age—thirty-five—and they grew up together. The oldest woman here just turned thirty, followed by me and the attorney candidate. We're both twenty-nine.

"She's not a hillbilly," I say. "Why are you always putting her down?"

Misty shakes her head. "Come on. These men are catches. Not only gorgeous and smart but freaking billionaires? The best the market has to offer. She's the type they sleep with once and then ghost. Not the type they're actually looking to settle down with."

While I don't like what she says about Ariel, I've wondered myself why men like these need Evangeline to find wives for them. But getting into any kind of an actual conversation with Misty seems pointless, so I let the comment slide.

Misty steps away from me. "See you around," she calls as she moves closer to the billionaire bachelors.

Misty's beautiful, but her attitude is pure poison. I certainly wasn't born with a bloody silver spoon up my arse. I worked hard to catch the eye of one of London's top designers. Two years ago, I moved to New York to open our American office. Evangeline reached out to me after reading an article about my career in *Vanity Fair*.

"Good evening, Emily."

The low timbre makes me tremble.

Sebastian Tate—the rock star—stands before me, holding two flutes of champagne. "Would you like a drink?"

I take the flute from him, willing my hands not to shake. "Lovely. Thank you."

Sebastian clinks his glass against mine.

I raise my eyebrows, waiting for him to make a toast. Instead, he takes a sip.

Odd, but I've learned to go with the flow here. Americans have their own way of doing things.

I follow suit and take a sip of the bubbly. It's a brut—dry, crisp, and delicious.

I wait for him to make conversation, but he doesn't. This is a man who writes song lyrics that win major awards, and he appears to have nothing to say to me.

I take another sip. "So...may I ask a question, Mr. Tate?"

He smiles. I can't help sucking in my breath. I've never been fond of long hair on a man, but... Wow. His is dark brown with a slight wave that's apparent even pulled back in a ponytail. As magnificent as it is, his eyes are the color of an aged whisky, and they seem to penetrate my flesh as he stares at me. I may burst into flames at any moment.

"Sebastian," he says.

"I'm sorry. What?"

"You called me Mr. Tate. My name is Sebastian. Or Seb if you prefer. And yes, you may ask me a question."

I take another sip of champagne, the bubbles tickling my nose as I tamp down a wave of nerves that seems determined to land between my thighs.

"Go ahead," he prompts.

I clear my throat. Why not be blunt? Evangeline told us to be ourselves, and Emily Kensington is as blunt as they come.

I flip my hair subtly—at least I hope it's subtle. "Why are you doing this? None of you need a matchmaker. Women undoubtedly flock to you. You're a celebrity, for goodness' sake. And...well...just look at you."

"I'd rather look at you."

I do my best to ignore the heat that his words ignite in me because I *do* want an answer. I'm truly curious.

"Are you going to answer my question, Mister... Sorry. Sebastian?"

He takes a sip, meets my gaze, and I try not to become hypnotized by those blazing eyes.

"There's no easy answer to that question, Emily."

"I didn't say I wanted an *easy* answer."

The slight smile he gives me carries only a hint of the sensuality of his last album cover, and yet, this close to him, I feel like the only woman in a stadium of millions. "When we read your bios and looked at your photos, you were the first woman I wanted to meet when we got here."

"Why?" I can't help asking, even though I know damned well he didn't answer my initial question. Already I've allowed myself to succumb to his flattery.

"Because I love a challenge."

"And you find me challenging? Just from reading about me?"

"I find you beguiling." Another sip. "And yes, challenging."

"Beguiling is an interesting word," I say. "Some would say it means charming or enchanting. Others would say a beguiling person has a deceptive quality. How do you mean it, Sebastian?"

He chuckles softly. "I know exactly what beguiling means, Emily. I write songs, remember?"

"You didn't answer my question." I raise an eyebrow. "Come to think of it, you didn't answer my first query either. Why are you doing this? You said I could ask."

He nods. "I did. But I never said I'd answer."

So he's playing that game. Good enough. I can play with the best of them. He thinks I'm beguiling? Fine. I'll be beguiling. I deliberately drop my gaze to the ground for a second and then look back up. "What if I answer a question for you?"

"What if you do?"

"Surely there must be something you'd like to know about me. Something that wasn't in the detailed biography Evangeline prepared. I'll answer honestly anything you ask... on the condition that you answer me honestly as well."

"How will you know I'm being honest?"

"I'll know." I burn him with my gaze.

"Very well. Why are *you* here, Emily?"

Is he bloody serious? Why *wouldn't* I be here? Why wouldn't any woman jump at the chance to live on a tropical island with all expenses paid? Gourmet food, excellent wine and liquor, new clothes, and the chance to meet four eligible bachelors looking for relationships? Nothing is required other than meeting the men. We don't have to get physical unless we want to, and we don't have to marry one, even if he asks. We don't have to do anything other than be here and meet them. Interact with them. As my assistant, Greta, would say, "It's a no brainer."

So I answer him honestly. Mostly honestly. "I'm here to meet you."

Sebastian's whisky eyes smolder. "You said you'd be honest."

"I *am* being honest." Just not wholly honest.

We're all here to meet the four of them. It's in the agreement. Everything else is icing on the cake—and we all know the icing is the best part.

"All right then. Here's the answer to your question. The first way."

I wrinkle my forehead. "What the hell does that mean?"

"You asked what I meant by beguiling. Charming? Or deceptive? I meant charming."

"You know exactly what question I want answered." I drain the last of the champagne from my flute. "Why, Sebastian? Why are you here? The real reason."

"First you answer another for me. Quid pro quo, right?"

I resist rolling my eyes. "Fine. What do you want to know?"

He takes a step toward me, closing the short distance between us. My skin heats. He's hardly my type, so why am I reacting this way?

"I want to know what makes you hot, Emily," he whispers. "What makes you wet? What makes you need to squeeze those luscious thighs together?"

I swallow, willing my legs not to turn to jelly.

"If I answer, you'll tell me what *I* want to know?"

"Yes. If you're honest with me about what makes you hot. What makes your flesh sizzle? What makes your knees weak? What turns you to melted butter, Emily?"

Easy enough for someone as blunt as I am.

"You do, Sebastian. Right now, at this moment, the answer is *you*."

He trails one finger over my cheek and down my jawline. Just that slight touch lights a fire between my legs.

"It's the truth? You're hot for me right now?"

Can't he tell? My chest is rosy and my nipples are straining against the flimsy fabric of my dress. "Yes. God, yes."

"Good. So good. Do you still want me to answer your question, Emily? Or would you rather I take you somewhere and fuck you against a wall?"

3
Guilty As Charged

Sienna

You never marry the rebound guy, no matter how rich and good looking he is.

Of course, these men go way beyond merely rich and good looking.

As usual, I'm the wallflower of the bunch. I feel like I'm back in high school—the gawky girl with braces who was still flat-chested at sixteen. Calling me a late bloomer is the understatement of the year. I got my braces off and finally filled out senior year, but by then no one noticed—or if they did, they didn't bother to include me in their already-formed cliques. I was forever the ugly duckling.

College, law school, a thriving career, and one broken engagement later, I'm that gawky girl in a sea of beautiful swans. Again.

I mean, we have an underwear model here for God's sake. How are any of us supposed to compete with that?

The answer? We're not supposed to compete at all.

"This isn't a competition," Evangeline said on day one. "You ladies are all spectacular, and I'm sure some friendships will be forged among you. But there are only four gentlemen and eight of you. It's possible the men won't fall in love with any of you. This is an experiment, so enjoy the fringe benefits."

Ginger walks toward me, carrying a plate of appetizers. "Aren't you eating?" she asks.

"Not hungry." I glance around the expansive outdoor courtyard. Palm trees line one side, and their fronds sway in the light tropical breeze. Tables and cocktail tables are scattered over the paved surface, and a full bar stands near the table of food. Despite feeling invisible, energy surges through me. I came here for a reason—to move forward with my life. To let go of negativity. "Seems two of the gentlemen have already found their targets for this evening."

"Targets?" Ginger laughs. "Seems that way. I have to say, I'm surprised."

Why?" I ask. "They're both gorgeous."

"So is everyone else here," Ginger says, taking a bite from a giant prawn.

"True enough." Though I'm not feeling the part.

Yup. I'm back in that stupid high school gymnasium,

standing against the wall, waiting to be asked to dance. I thought I'd outgrown that wallflower feeling, but here it is again.

I forgot how much I hated it.

Evangeline Livingston scurries toward Ginger and me. "Ladies, come with me. I want to introduce you to Alex."

Alex Maxwell is the bestselling author of the Nash Beckett thriller series. I've never read any of them, but each book hits number one as soon as it's released, and the series has spawned a multi-million dollar film franchise. I've never seen the movies, either.

"Aren't we supposed to wait until he comes to us?" I ask.

"Alex is shy," she says. "He's a bit of a recluse. I'm going to prod him along."

"Why us?" Ginger asks.

"The two of you are the most suited to him, I think. He has a master of fine arts and a Ph.D. in literature. You two are both well educated."

"What about Rachel?" Ginger gestures. "She's a physicist."

"She's not..." Evangeline bites her lower lip, as if she's struggling to find the right words. "Just come with me, please."

Why not? I'm here to meet these four men. That's the whole point. I look down at the clingy gold number that Evangeline insists brings out my eyes—which are light brown, not gold—and my toes that are painted the same color and showcased in strappy sandals that make me feel way more *Legally Blonde* than I ever wanted to.

Ginger and I follow Evangeline to a cocktail table where Alex Maxwell nurses a drink that looks like bourbon or scotch. He's the most brooding of the bunch, though they all have a certain darkness about them. Alex is dressed in a black suit and white shirt, no tie. Around his neck hangs a thin gold chain. Understated and sexy. His brown hair swoops over his forehead in an unruly wave.

"Alex"—Evangeline holds out her hand—"I'd like to introduce Ginger Swanson and Sienna Costello."

Introduce? He already knows who we are, what we do, and practically how many pisses we take a day. Okay, not that last part, but the introductory bios Evangeline prepared about us were pretty explicitly detailed.

"Good evening, ladies." Alex raises his eyebrows, showcasing gorgeous gold-green irises, but he doesn't smile.

Does this man even want to be here?

As far as I understand, Alex and his buddies are footing the bill for the eight of us to stay on this private island. I assume they paid for the makeovers, the travel costs, the food...everything. I'm not sure what the billionaires expect, but... Doesn't he want his money's worth?

"Nice to meet you." Ginger holds out her hand.

Alex shakes it formally. "Dr. Swanson. The dermatologist."

"Yes."

"And you're Ms. Costello. The attorney."

"Guilty as charged." Whoa! That's the same line I used when I met my ex. It just popped out.

That gets his lips to curve upward, but only slightly. It did the same for my ex, and we ended up hitting it off, getting engaged, and then—

"Congratulations on your most recent bestseller," Ginger says, interrupting my thoughts.

He smiles more broadly this time. "Thank you. Do you ladies need a refill?" He nods to our champagne flutes.

"Not for me yet." I gesture to his drink. "Don't you like champagne?"

"Not especially. I'm a bourbon man."

I nod. "I like bourbon too."

"Indeed? What's your favorite?"

I'm supposed to have a favorite? Whatever the bartender brings me, usually. "Four Roses." It's the first one I could think of.

"Four Roses is nice, though it's a blend, which makes a flavor profile difficult."

"What do you like?" I ask.

He brings his glass to his lips, takes a sip. "This is Angel's Envy. It's aged in port wine barrels which gives it notes of fruit and spice. It's one of my favorites. Would you like to try it?"

"Uh...sure." I take the glass from him and take a sip.

And oh my God...

The liquor dances across my tongue. It's that good. The oak from the barrel mingles with the slight sweetness of the port and the irresistible smoky caramel of the bourbon itself. I swallow, and it warms my throat without the least bit of harshness going down.

"What do you think?" he asks.

"I think that may be the best thing I've ever had in my mouth."

Ginger lifts her eyebrows playfully. "You sure about that?"

Ginger is a classic beauty with dark hair and emerald-colored eyes. She's also a world class flirt, apparently. My cheeks burn at her suggestion.

Alex doesn't seem fazed by Ginger's innuendo. "If you like this, you have to try Pappy Van Winkle's. It makes this taste like rotgut."

"I highly doubt that."

"Want to bet? Come to the bar. I'll show you."

"Okay. Come on, Ginger."

She smiles. "You two go ahead." She finishes her champagne, grabs another from a server passing by with a tray of flutes, and leaves the table.

"Excuse me a minute," I say to Alex.

He nods.

I catch up with Ginger and grab her arm. "Why are you leaving me alone with him?"

"Because three's a crowd. Go for it, Sienna. He's obviously into you."

"We both like bourbon. That hardly makes us soulmates."

"Who's looking for a soulmate? For God's sake, would you try to have fun? Forget about Link or Leon or whatever his name was."

"Leroy. His name was Leroy." And we were together for four years, engaged for two. The wedding was supposed to be two months from now.

"Whatever. He was an idiot to let you go, and now you're on an island full of billionaires."

"Four billionaires isn't exactly an island full."

"It's more than you've seen in one place before, I bet. Let your hair down."

"Maybe he's not my type."

"Gorgeous, wealthy, and well-endowed isn't your type?"

My cheeks warm. "We don't know if he's well-endowed."

"Are you kidding me? He radiates big dick energy. Dark

and brooding and raw sexy. I'll bet he's fucking eight inches. You can let me know later."

"Are you insane? I just met the man." My belly flutters despite my words.

"You think he's not gunning to get one of us in the sack? Why else are these men here? They want to get to know each one of us...and I'm sure that means in the biblical sense."

"Evangeline said—"

"Yes, I know what Evangeline said. We're not obligated to do anything physical with them. But no one's going to buy a cow without sampling the milk first. Now get your firm little ass back there before Alex loses interest." She gives me a soft shove and then walks away.

I draw in a breath and walk over to the bar where Alex waits with two lowball glasses.

He hands one to me, his green-gold gaze burning into me.

"Take a sip, Sienna," he says, his voice a husky rasp. "And then tell me if Angel's Envy is the best thing you've ever had in your mouth."

I bring the glass to my lips—

Alex moves toward me, his breath hot against my earlobe. "And trust me. By the end of the evening, no bourbon will be the best thing you've ever tasted."

A NOTE FROM HELEN

Dear Reader,

Thank you for reading *Volatile Vice*. If you want to find out about my current backlist and future releases, please visit my website, like my Facebook page, and join my mailing list. If you're a fan, please join my Facebook street team (Hardt & Soul) to help spread the word about my books. I regularly do awesome giveaways for my street team members.

If you enjoyed the story, please take the time to leave a review. I welcome all feedback.

I wish you all the best!

Helen

Sign up for my newsletter here:

http://www.helenhardt.com/signup

ALSO BY HELEN HARDT

Standalones

My Heart Still Beats

Misadventures with a Rock Star

Misadventures of a Good Wife (with Meredith Wild)

Bellamy Brothers

Savage Sin

Sweet Sin

Seductive Sin

Vengeful Vice

Volatile Vice

Victorious Vice

Follow Me Series

Follow Me Darkly

Follow Me Under

Follow Me Always

Darkly

Under

Black Rose Series

Blush

Bloom

Blossom

Wolfes of Manhattan

Rebel

Recluse

Runaway

Rake

Reckoning

Escape

Moonstone

Raven

Garnet

Buck

Opal

Phoenix

Amethyst

Sex and the Season

Lily and the Duke

Rose in Bloom

Lady Alexandra's Lover

Sophie's Voice

The Perils of Patricia

Steel Brothers Saga

Craving

Obsession

Possession

Melt

Burn

Surrender

Shattered

Twisted

Unraveled

Breathless

Ravenous

Insatiable

Fate

Legacy

Descent

Awakened

Cherished

Freed

Spark

Flame

Blaze

Smolder

Flare

Scorch

Chance

Fortune

Destiny

Melody

Harmony

Encore

Blood Bond Saga

Unchained

Unhinged

Undaunted

Unmasked

Undefeated

Temptation Saga

Tempting Dusty

Teasing Annie

Taking Catie

Taming Angelina

Treasuring Amber

Trusting Sydney

Tantalizing Maria

The Billion Heirs (with Vanessa Vale)

Scarred

Flawed

Broken

Non-Fiction

got style?

Cooking with Hardt & Soul

Auf Deutsch:

Wolfes of Manhattan

Rebel

Recluse

Runaway

Rake

Reckoning

En français:

La série Steel Brothers:

Attraction

Obsession

Possession

Turbulence

Effervescence

Résilience

Déflagration

Aliénation

Révélation

Les Wolfe de Manhattan

Rebelle

Reclus

ACKNOWLEDGMENTS

Thank you so much to my editor (and son!) Eric J. McConnell; my beta readers, Corinne Akers, Serena Drummond, Karen Aguilera, and Linda Dunn; my cover artist, Amanda Shepard of Shepard Originals; and my audiobook narrators, Eric J. McConnell and Kaileigh Riess. You all helped *Vengeful Vice* shine!

ABOUT THE AUTHOR

#1 *New York Times*, #1 *USA Today*, and #1 *Wall Street Journal* bestselling author Helen Hardt's passion for the written word began with the books her mother read to her at bedtime. She wrote her first story at age six and hasn't stopped since. In addition to being an award-winning author of romantic fiction, she's a mother, an attorney, a black belt in Taekwondo, a grammar geek, an appreciator of fine red wine, and a lover of Ben and Jerry's ice cream. She writes from her home in Colorado, where she lives with her family. Helen loves to hear from readers.

Please sign up for her newsletter here:
http://www.helenhardt.com/signup
Visit her here:
http://www.helenhardt.com

Printed in Great Britain
by Amazon

60859637R00180